The witch snapped his fingers, and the curtains at one end of the room drew themselves back. A man and a woman, dressed all in black, were tied on the floor in the far alcove.

"Visitors," said Talivane with theatrical pleasure. "From the Duke."

Naiji said coldly, "He hires Spirits, now. What next?"

Her brother shrugged and quoted, *"All's fair in war with witches."*

The prisoners' clothing was that of M—

Ace Fantasy books by Will Shetterly

CATS HAVE NO LORD
LIAVEK *(edited with Emma Bull)*
WITCH BLOOD

WITCH BLOOD

WILL SHETTERLY

ACE FANTASY BOOKS
NEW YORK

This book is an Ace Fantasy
original edition, and has never
been previously published.

WITCH BLOOD

An Ace Fantasy Book/published by arrangement with
the author and the author's agent, Valerie Smith

PRINTING HISTORY
Ace Fantasy edition/March 1986

ISBN: 0-441-89644-8

Ace Fantasy Books are published by The Berkley Publishing Group,
200 Madison Avenue, New York, New York 10016.
PRINTED IN THE UNITED STATES OF AMERICA

This book is for Emma Bull, my wife and my love

WITCH BLOOD

◈ 1 ◈

MY DAUGHTER'S VILLA

I WOKE EARLY this morning. The winter sun had yet to rise from the sea, though I heard gulls chiding her to hurry. A bowl of cinnamon and dried bay leaves sat near my pallet, and their scent was thick in the closed sleeping room. I lay beneath the soft cotton quilt that my second wife had made for our wedding bed. I closed my eyes and tried to sleep again, but I could not. I remembered the people and events of my life.

When I was a boy in the western fishing village of Loh, which means *more than two homes* in that language, I was chosen by a wandering priest of the White Mountain School of the Warrior-Saint to master her Art. Only one part of the Art will I claim to have learned well, and that is the art of memory. Sometimes I think it is my curse, and sometimes, my blessing. This morning it was both. Enemies and friends, some lost to death and some to time, came before me to say, "Rifkin. In our way, we touched. It is important. Never forget."

Old Tassi hobbled into my room with the sun. I had dressed in white trousers, a scarlet jerkin, black sandals, and a black

1

sash, but I still lay on the pallet with my eyes closed.

"Wake, good Rifkin!" She threw open the curtains and gave me her broadest toothless smile. "It's a beautiful morning!"

"It's grey and cold," I said.

"Yes, good Rifkin," she agreed with several nods. "Your daughter waits in the morning room. Cook has prepared your favorite breakfast, poached ostrich eggs in goat's milk and—"

"No," I said.

"Oh, yes," she said. "And yesterday's ship brought oranges, so—"

"I'll have yogurt," I said. "With a few nuts and raisins. And a glass of water. Served in the garden."

"But—"

"Please, Tassi."

"Very well." She left shaking her head. "You're going to hurt Cook's feelings, you know."

I went down to the gardens and ate my bowl of yogurt, nuts, and raisins while I watched the sea. Cook had added coconut and bananas to the yogurt, and a cup of green tea sat beside the water pitcher, but I did not complain. The waves rolled in under a windy, colorless sky. As I finished my breakfast, Feschiani joined me, carrying the scrolls of the latest census under her arm. I said, "I'm going wandering."

"Oh?" she said. "Where?"

"Wandering, daughter. If I knew where, it would hardly be wandering."

"For long?"

I stood and shrugged.

"Who'll you take with you?"

"No one."

"You have a duty," she said, setting the scrolls aside to link my arm with hers.

I said, "No, Feschiani. You have duties now."

She only shook her head, reminding me too much of her mother, and said, "You owe something to our people."

"Fine. Pay them from the treasury."

"That's not funny, Pipa."

I realized then that I should simply have left a note and gone. I kissed her forehead, an effect which is spoiled since I have to stand on tiptoe. "What do I owe them?"

"Your knowledge, Pipa."

"No one's ever thought much of it."

"That's not so, Pipa!"

"Maybe not," I said. "But you rule now."

She glanced at me from the corners of her eyes and said slyly, "Which means you obey me?"

No, I should have left without a note. "Well . . ."

"Please, Pipa."

"You think I'm too old to travel?"

I expected her to answer *Not in body,* but she is not that much like her mother. Or perhaps she is subtler. She said immediately, "No, Pipa. I think, however, that you should write down your story before you go. For the people. And for me."

"That'll take months!"

She smiled, quite pleased with herself. "I know."

"Write?" I said.

"Yes."

"Pay a feast-singer for some lies. Pay the feast-singer well, and you'll get very good lies."

"Pipa, please. For me?"

Well, this is a cold winter. I'll stay in the warmth of our villa with no worse enemies than pens and ink and virgin parchment. But when these foes have been broken, dispersed, and defiled, Rifkin Wanderer will wander again.

2

THE MOUNTAINS
OF THE KOND

I PAUSED AT a fork in the mountain road, wondering which branch would take me farther from Istviar and the sea. Both led north. Both were narrow tracks of half-frozen mud and slush. Neither appeared to have been used since winter fled these hills. A sign of bleached and broken wood was half hidden by a leafless bush. It said *Gromandiel* in the language of the Kond, but I did not know if this was a queen, a god, the nearest mountain, a village, an inn, or an obscene suggestion. When a sudden puff of wind sent a leaf racing to the left, I pretended that it was an omen and followed it.

Perhaps it was my weariness from three days of hiking without food or shelter, or perhaps it was the fault of the fading light of dusk, or perhaps I saw the clump of white in the path as a large patch of snow. I did not recognize the bear until it stood. Its coat was long and very clean. Its eyes were pale blue. My axe felt much heavier in my hands as we stared. When the bear growled softly and padded closer, I glanced around for refuge or aid. The woods were bleak in twilight.

The oaks were naked and grey, almost malevolent. I could try to scale one before the bear charged, but try was all I would do.

The bear's paws made soft sucking sounds on the muddy road. I shifted my axe to my left hand, letting my right settle on the hilt of my short sword. The bear growled loudest as it attacked. I stepped forward, drawing my short sword and sweeping the axe before me. The bear reared high overhead. A heavy paw descended toward my face. I threw myself to one side, thrusting the short sword at the bear's stomach. My axe bit into its foreleg, but in the beast's hunger or anger, it never noticed. Its other paw came down to rake my chest.

I had no time to note my wounds. I brought the back edge of my double-bladed axe up into the bear's crotch. It shrieked, as I had expected, but it did not curl up as a human might. The bear, while it stood, was half again my height. My only hope of survival was to get close enough to pierce its heart or brain.

I feinted for its head, then chopped at its thigh. As my axe burrowed deep into its flesh, its paw came down on my helmet, scraping against leather and iron, then shredding my shoulder. I almost lost consciousness. Still, out of reflex or the many years of training, I slashed blindly with the short sword while I fell. I don't know where I struck it, but my blow kept the bear from throwing itself on me. I rolled through the mud and came up standing.

The bear raced after me. I was past the point of conscious thought. My legs moved of their own accord, and I was running toward the bear as if to embrace it. At the moment when its forelegs would close around me, my right hand rose and I darted aside. The sword jarred home, though the shock wrenched it from my grip. I spun about, bringing my axe to my right hand, and with my left, slipped a dagger from its sheath on my belt. In my mind I rehearsed the death song, but when I looked at the bear, I saw that I would sing for it, not for myself. My short sword protruded from its left eye.

The bear lay in the road like a dirty, abandoned bale. A tremor shook it for an instant as its soul escaped, then it was only a bag of poor fur and stringy meat. I was cold and sad and my chest felt as though someone had sown it with hot coal.

I wanted to collapse where I stood. My weapons fell from my numb hands into the half-frozen mud. I thought I would follow, but I managed to stumble the few, short steps to the bear's side. "Forgive me, Brother Bear," I whispered. "We shouldn't have met here." I thought I would die, and I was relieved.

Applause came from the woods behind me. "Soldier!" a woman called in Kondish. "Well done! Very well done!"

She watched from forty paces away in the shadow of an elm. As I jerked my short sword from the bear's eye, I saw that the woman's weapons were a pearl-handled dagger at her belt and a longbow of ash held casually by her side. The dim light had helped to hide her, as had her appearance. Her hair, clipped close above her shoulders, was as white as the bear. Her skin was little darker than cream. She wore a birchbark quiver on one shoulder, and her jacket and boots were of silver fox fur. Her pants were of some rare white leather. If a woman made of ice had died, this might be her ghost.

"Greetings, Lady." I nodded politely and looked for hidden companions. "Are you..." I had to pause for breath, which made me wonder again about my wounds. "...separated from a hunting party?"

"You might say that."

Her smile reminded me that I still held my short sword. Feeling foolish, I lowered its point and said, "I hear these hills aren't safe to travel in alone."

"As you begin to learn?"

I shrugged, though it cost me strength. "So it seems."

"These woods are safe enough for me."

"You're lucky the bear didn't catch your scent."

"Old Avo wouldn't have hurt me."

"He was your pet?" I stared at her. "You might have called him off."

"I didn't see the need in time. I thought he would win."

"And now?" I lifted the sword again.

"You're afraid of me?" She laughed. "That's rather flattering. Wise, too, but still flattering." In spite of her white hair, her face was young. She might have seen twenty-five summers, but certainly no more. Ignoring my sword, she said, "Are you wounded badly?"

"I've never been wounded well."

She smiled, baring bright teeth. The front two protruded slightly, like a rabbit's. She said, "You're amusing."

"I'll probably bleed to death soon," I said, "if I don't laugh myself to death first." I let the tip of my sword drop again. If she intended to complete the bear's work, she would have nocked an arrow to her bow and shot me before I saw her.

"Don't worry, little warrior. I'll help you." She pointed at the grey corpse of a tree that had fallen across the road some years before and been dragged aside so a cart could pass. "Sit. And take off those rags." She gestured at my shirt and jacket. I glanced at her to see what she intended, but I learned nothing from her face. She set aside her bow, slipped the quiver of arrows from her shoulder, and said, "Go on. I'll heal you."

She carried no healer's kit that I could see. I said, "You're a witch?"

"Yes. Toss your sword over there." She indicated a spot near the bear's corpse where I had dropped my other weapons.

I think I can say that even when I was a child and heard the tales of the old Empire, I never hated the witchfolk. Some people are tall, some have light skin, some are witchborn. Yet I knew very well that iron and steel were the only things that repelled magic, and I have never liked being at another's mercy.

The woman smiled. Her eyes were the green of the sea on a stormy day, and her lips were as lush as appleberries in summer. She said, "If I wanted you to die, I'd only have to leave you here. True?"

"True," I said. "But why would you help me after I killed your guard?"

"Perhaps because you killed him. My brother and I need fighters." Eyeing my patched clothing, she added, "You seem to need a rich master."

"I need a physician." I threw my short sword beside my axe and dagger, then slumped back on the log.

"Lean forward," she said. With a grimace of distaste, she tugged off my helmet to toss it beside my weapons. Peeling the fragments of cloth from my torn chest, she said, "There's no other iron on you?"

"My belt."

"Ah." Her fingers were gentle at my waist as she uncinched the buckle and pulled the belt from me. It joined my helmet. "That's all?"

"My boots."

"Your boots?"

"Steel studs."

"Oh." She tugged each from my feet and said nothing about the holes in my socks. "Anything more?"

"You will heal me?"

I heard a trace of annoyance in her answer. "I've said so."

"There's a stiletto strapped to the inside of my thigh."

She grinned as she pulled off my pants. "You aren't very trusting, are you?"

Naked then, I said, "I also keep a long pin hidden in my hair."

She found the throwing needle behind my fisherman's top-knot, and her eyes went wide. "Are you a soldier or an assassin?"

"I'm cautious. And I may be dying, Lady." My limbs were so weak that I might not have been able to lift them. The evening's cool air was lulling me toward something deeper than sleep.

"That's all of your supplies?"

I nodded my head, which helped to wake me. "All, Lady."

She stood before me. "Will you serve me loyally, until my word or my death releases you?"

I looked up into her face. I knew that I would not be able to leave this place alone and that I would not survive the night if she left me. "This is your price for healing?"

"It is," she said with obvious satisfaction.

I had no idea who she was or what she wanted from me, yet I whispered, "Then I will serve you loyally."

"Good. Who are you, my boundman?" she asked.

"I'm Rifkin. Rifkin Wayfarer." I could not see her face to tell if that name meant anything to her.

"I am Naiji Gromandiel, Rifkin. I promise food, shelter, and clothing for you and your kin, so long as you serve me well."

Perhaps I should have been happy then. Since I served her, she would heal me and care for me, and perhaps her home would become the home that I had lost when I fled Istviar. But I shivered as I heard her words. Her tone told me that she knew she did not need to speak the second part of the vow: *I promise death for you and all you love, if ever you betray me.*

I said, "Fine. Heal me, Lady."

She laughed. "You won't be the most submissive boundman who's sworn himself to me." She reached out to lift my chin, saying, "Look into my eyes, my Rifkin."

I looked up again. Her eyes caught light from the setting sun. Her irises seemed cold, turquoise plates. She held my gaze for a long moment, then nodded. "I do not join with you to heal you, Rifkin," she said. "I join with you to help you heal yourself. Do you understand that?"

I nodded.

"Do you trust me, then?"

What choice did I have? I nodded.

"Good. Follow my lead, and you'll be well. Do you believe me?"

And I had to believe her. I nodded again.

"Good." She let her fingers slide from my temples to my bearded cheek. "Then do not think, Rifkin. You know something of meditation?"

"A little."

"Good. Then let your mind accept your body's suggestions." She began to massage my face. As her fingers danced, my pain subsided. When her hands descended to my neck, it was as though lightning touched me. I gasped, thinking I could not bear the pleasure of her fingertips and knowing I did not want her to move her hands away. The sensation was much like the first time a lover had touched me intimately, and my skin had tingled with something more intense than tickling.

She saw my reaction and her caress changed, stroking more firmly where she had previously teased. She traced a path along my torso that followed my ribs and hips, ignoring the bear's gouges. My breath deepened. She moved her hands along my hips, and I sighed.

"You like that?" she whispered.

"Very much."

"Concentrate on the sensation."

"I doubt I could concentrate on anything else."

When she smiled, I noted her slightly protruding front teeth and thought them surprisingly attractive. She saw something in my expression and said, "You feel stronger?"

"Yes," I replied, though what I felt was closer to lazy comfort than strength. My muscles, answering her ministrations, relaxed. I forgot my wounds in the pleasure of the moment. I was not reminded of pain until she touched the lowest gouge in my chest, and I gasped.

"Think of warmth," Naiji said. "Think of strength."

"I'm thinking of razors," I said, "and sea water poured on open sores."

"Think of warmth," she repeated. Her hand moved down to circle my navel. One finger left a trail of sticky, drying blood.

"Warmth." I sighed and closed my eyes. My hands lay limp on her shoulders. Then something cold and slushy slapped against my stomach. Shocked, I jerked forward.

She was washing me with snow. "Warmth," she said, admonishing and amused.

The hand that cupped snow cleaned my chest. No blood flowed where her fingers passed. She said, "You're stronger than you think, Rifkin. Use that strength." Her hands followed the paths the bear had carved. My wounds felt like a track for fire gods.

The magic almost fled when I realized that someone watched us. I knew this suddenly, without knowing how I knew. I scanned the bony shadows of the trees. No one was there. I thought of a witch watching with mindsight, and I thought I concealed my fear.

Naiji said, "Something?"

The notion was ridiculous. The bare elms hid no one. My exile had made me too suspicious. The distraction brought back hints of pain and cold, and I prayed the interruption would not end my healing. "No."

"Find the warmth, then," Naiji said. "Don't forget. The warmth!"

"Yes," I said, suddenly breathless. I felt heat across the wounds in my chest, heat about my entire body as though I had been transported to the beach at Loh in a summer afternoon. As Naiji massaged me, the places of heat grew closer to each other. I wondered what would happen when my entire body seemed consumed by fires of magic.

"Now!" Naiji said.

"Now!" I cried aloud, echoing her as, for a long moment, we shared something more intimate than any pleasure-making between friends.

Sometime later she laughed, then stood and gathered my clothes to throw them at me. "I've chosen well."

"I'm glad you think so . . . I think. For what?"

"You'll learn soon enough."

"I'd like some answers."

"You'll have them soon enough, my Rifkin. Dress yourself."

It was not until I began to fasten my shirt that I noticed that all signs of my fight with the bear had left my body. Only the scars of older encounters remained to say that I had ever been wounded in battle.

I dressed quickly, and was trying to rub the bloodstains from my clothes with a handful of snow when Naiji said, "Follow." Without a backward glance at me or the bear's corpse, she strode off on a deer trail that appeared to climb the nearest hill.

"Where do we go?" I said, hurrying after her. Night was upon us, and only a faint band of pink remained in the western sky to salute the coming evening.

"To Castle Gromandiel."

"The road doesn't pass it?"

"Not close. This is faster."

I tried to accept the oddities of the north, but I was suspicious of any castle so insignificant as to be bypassed by a merchant's route. I looked back at the bear's pale form and thought of other things that might stalk the woods at night. "The road would be safer."

Naiji halted and laughed. "No place in this valley is safer than with me, though that may not be safe enough for either of us." She turned on her heel and set off into the trees.

We walked in silence for half an hour or more. Her night sight was better than mine, or else she had memorized the path's features. She never faltered or stumbled. I tripped in holes and over branches more times than I would care to count, but I had learned to catch myself quickly when I was a novice in the ways of the Art. As we hiked through the barren trees, the moon rose, missing only a tiny sliver of his full self. A wolf barked four times from far away, and Naiji turned so quickly to glance for it that she almost fell. I reached to steady her, but she pushed me away and said, "You'll treat me as your master, except when I say otherwise. Understand, Rifkin Boundman?"

"No. I swore to serve you, Naiji Gromandiel. I never swore to obey your whims."

"What?" She glared at me, then grinned. "I'm bringing my brother a lawyer, not a fighter, I see."

"You've brought your brother no one, Lady. I swore to serve you, not him."

"Among the Kond, Rifkin, the vow means—"

"Along the Ladizhar, a vow means what it says. And no more."

She tapped my chest with her index finger. "You've traveled far from that sea, Rifkin."

I met her gaze. "You may release me from your service, if you prefer."

"There's only one release from my service."

"My death?"

"Yes."

"No," I noted. "There are at least two paths to my freedom, my lady. The second is through *your* death."

She stared at me for a long moment. "Do you threaten—"

"Never. I swore to serve you. But if ever I'm unable to save you from danger, Lady, I'll be free again."

She smiled, almost fondly. "Ah, Rifkin. You aren't comfortable in the inferior's role, are you?"

"I might not be, if I'd accepted an inferior's role. Your word binds you to me as closely as mine binds me to you."

"You speak rather insolently, my Rifkin, for a foreigner and a boundman."

"I do so in your interest, Lady, as best as I can evaluate your interest."

"And I suppose you won't accept another's estimate of my best interest?"

"No."

"Not even my own?"

"Especially not your own, Lady."

She reached out to squeeze my hand. "Try not to make this difficult for either of us, hmm?"

"And you, the same."

"Yes," she said. "Definitely a lawyer. Come on, lawyer. We've rested long enough."

I followed her for another twenty minutes or so. We left the path and climbed through brush and scree up a hill so steep that we had to use our hands to steady ourselves. Naiji paused midway to what seemed a sheer rock face, pointed upward, and said, "Your new home, Rifkin."

Far above us a castle jutted up from the high cliff like a shark's tooth. The mountain towered over it, shading the castle from the moonlight, so all I could see was the silhouette against the starry sky. My impression was that Naiji's keep was huge and old and possibly carved from the rock rather than built upon it. Perhaps Castle Gromandiel had been grown magically from the stone.

She seemed to expect me to comment. "It appears, ah, very defensible," I said.

"No one's ever conquered it." There was enough pride in her voice that I did not ask why anyone would want to take a castle, however formidable, that stood on a forgotten cliff in the midst of wild woods and bleak hills. After all, whatever I might think of it, she was right. It was my new home.

3

CASTLE GROMANDIEL

NAIJI WAS CONTENT to stand and admire her home. I said, "How do we reach the top? Scaling cliffs in the dark isn't an art I know."

"Like this." She led me to the base of the bare rock face, then cupped her hands about her mouth and made a call like a mountain cat's. "Step back." She drew me beneath a slight overhang, and a thick braid of knotted hemp fell nearby. "Can you climb a rope?"

"I can climb any line."

"Good." Naiji went first, disappearing in the shadow of the cliff. I tucked the shaft of my axe into my belt, then followed her. My arms ached before I had climbed a third of the rope's length, but there was no way to rest other than clinging to the rope, so I continued.

Naiji's fox-fur boots were the first sight to greet my eyes as I clambered over the cliff's edge. Next to them were two huge boots made of moosehide, large enough that someone might have decided to dress a statue, as is sometimes done in the temples of the island nations. Doubting this was the case, I felt very vulnerable as I looked up.

The man beside Naiji was immense, even for a Kond. His hair had been cut around his head so that in the night, he seemed to wear half of a coconut for a helmet. A tangled pale beard sprouted from his face like smoke. His clothes—baggy pants and a hooded jacket—appeared to have been sewn from old woolen blankets. A long straight sword at his hip would have been wielded with both hands by a normal warrior.

He moved his fist to indicate me and said in an oddly high-pitched voice, "Kill him, mistress?"

Naiji reached up to pat the giant's shoulder. "No, Avarineo. He's to be your friend."

The man shook his head. "Friend? No, mistress. He smells of death."

"That's not his fault," Naiji answered. "He was trapped in the woods by one of our defenders. You would have done the same, Avarineo."

The giant stared, and I wished there was something behind me besides a long fall to the rocks. I knew I could never free my axe from my belt before he attacked, if he chose to. I doubted it would be much use, if I could.

"Which did he kill, mistress?"

Naiji glanced at me in warning, then said, "It wasn't his fault, Avarineo. Truly."

"Which?"

"Old Avo," she answered sadly.

The giant's fists bunched together like boulders, but Naiji interposed herself between us before he could act. "No! He didn't know that you and Avo were spirit-brothers! Avo threatened him. I saw it!"

"You saw it, mistress?" The man's voice carried his anguish. "You did not help?"

"I thought Avo could handle him. I was wrong. I'm sorry, Avarineo. Truly."

The giant pointed at me and growled, "You will never be my friend. Never."

"Yes, he will," Naiji said. "He must be. We can't afford to fight among ourselves. He'll be your friend. Understand, Avarineo? He will be your friend."

"He will never be my friend. I'll kill him, mistress. He is

bad. Very bad." Avarineo reached for my throat with a massive, gnarled hand.

"I didn't know the bear was your brother," I said, as calmly as I could. "He attacked me. I did not attack him."

"True?" The giant paused a step from me with his fingers much too near my skin.

"True!" Naiji put both her hands against the giant's beard. "I saw."

"I wish to be your friend," I said.

"You'll never be my friend," Avarineo growled, but with less conviction. He let his arms drop to his sides. His stare continued as though he hoped his gaze would push me off the cliff.

Naiji suddenly embraced him. "Then pretend he's your friend. For my sake." Releasing him, she said, "Please, Avarineo?"

"For your sake," he said. "But I only pretend." He pointed again at me. "You are not really my friend, man."

"His name is Rifkin."

"Hah!" said Avarineo. "A stupid name."

I said, "It was considered a good one in Istviar."

"It may be a good name in some stupid land. Not here."

"Maybe not," I said. "But it's mine."

"You should change it," said Avarineo. "To something less stupid."

I nodded. "I'll remember your advice."

"Your name sounds like a fart," said the giant.

"Avarineo!" Naiji said.

"Sorry, mistress."

"Truly?"

"Well . . ." He looked at the ground. "It's not my fault his name sounds like a fart."

"You're trying to start a fight," Naiji said.

Avarineo looked up and nodded. "Yes, mistress."

"Don't. Pretend Rifkin's your friend. Remember that."

"I will remember that." He had bowed his head before Naiji, but he glanced down at me. "I will also remember Avo."

"Fine," Naiji said with considerable annoyance. "Remember Avo. But protect Rifkin. He's bound to me."

The giant's jaw gaped.

"Close your mouth, old friend."

"But, mistress . . ."

"Yes?"

"He killed Avo!"

"Yes. And fairly."

"He is small. Very small."

"He fights better than Avo did. Can you say the same?"

"He is funny-looking."

"He's darker than our folk. He was born that way."

"His name sounds like a fart!"

She sighed. "I tire of this, Avarineo. Haul up the rope. We don't need to be attacked while we argue."

He stared blankly, then nodded. "Yes, mistress." He bent, and his arms moved with the precision of clockwork as he pulled up the line we had climbed.

"I could build a machine to make that task easier," I said. "A winch and a pulley . . ." I considered this for a second or two. "And perhaps rig it to a rope ladder, rather than a single strand . . ."

Naiji laughed. "You are full of surprises! Not a lawyer, but an engineer, eh?"

"I've learned a few tricks," I said modestly.

"Obviously," she answered, pleased. "But for that"—she jerked her chin to indicate the giant's task—"we have Avarineo. It makes him feel useful."

"And if you no longer had him?"

She hesitated, then said, "Then we'd chain two slaves here, and let them serve us."

"I see."

She glanced at me, so I could not pretend to mistake her warning. "You could be one of them."

"No, thanks."

"Done, mistress," Avarineo announced.

"Good."

"Kill him?" he said hopefully, jerking his thumb at me.

"No! And don't ask again."

Abashed, he said, "Yes, mistress."

She looked at me. "Offer him your hand."

I looked at Avarineo, who glowered with mixed suspicion and confusion. "What do you mean?"

"It's a way of showing trust."

"I'm not sure I have any to show."

"I can't be worrying that one of you will kill the other. Offer your hand, Rifkin."

I flexed my fingers, since this might be my last chance to do so, and held out my left.

"The right," said Naiji.

Reluctantly, I obeyed.

Avarineo stared at my hand, then grinned.

"Don't hurt him," Naiji ordered.

His grin disappeared. His voice was like that of a child who had been slapped. "No, mistress." His great hand enclosed mine. I slid my palm up so that my thumb could press under his, if I had to. The giant was content to squeeze gently, and then he released me.

"We are friends?" I asked.

"We are not enemies," he said.

"That pleases me."

"It is odd not to be enemies with a man whose name sounds like a fart."

"Avarineo!" Naiji said.

I only laughed, since his insult had no threat behind it.

"Come, Rifkin," said Naiji. "My brother waits."

The castle was even larger than it had seemed from below. I suspected that it might easily garrison five hundred soldiers, so long as supplies could be brought to them. I wondered again why anyone would think this valley so important. I had journeyed from a Kondish city that was too small to threaten anyone, where no one seemed to suspect that this fortress existed, and I was told that the city beyond the hills was no greater or any more ambitious.

We walked along a trail wide enough for two horses to pass. After a moment Naiji stopped and said, "Be careful of Avarineo. Though he's simple, he has a long memory."

"So do I. But I'll try to make friends with him."

"Good. Now, another matter."

"Yes?"

"My brother will want to know your history."

"And you don't?"

"I know what's important about you, Rifkin. You're competent, and you're true to your word."

"I might leave this place while everyone sleeps."

"No."

"Why not?"

"It wouldn't be easy to escape our keep. Avarineo guards the cliff most nights, and someone always watches the supply road. Besides, I learned a little about your nature while healing you."

I said, "I see."

Something must have told her that I was not pleased. Naiji set her hand on my arm. "I only assured myself that you honor your vows."

I shrugged as if it did not matter.

She released my arm. "So, what'll you tell my brother?"

"I'll admit that I'm an exiled prince who roams these lands in hopes of raising an army to free his native country. What else could I say?"

She glanced at me before she laughed. "Right."

"You're too perceptive, Lady. I'm actually a simple fellow who lived peaceably near his village until he learned of a great evil in the world and reluctantly set out to make everything right again."

Naiji shook her head. "My brother has no sense of humor, Rifkin."

"Then I shouldn't tell him I'm a disguised magician who travels to escape his enemies?"

"You carry too much iron for him to ever believe that."

"Oh. Will he accept that I'm a wandering mercenary who recently took the wrong side in a war, and therefore seeks a new master?"

"Perhaps. Though he may wonder how you came to play mercenary. You seem too intelligent and too well educated to be a common soldier."

"Did I say I was a common soldier?" I scratched my forehead under my helmet. "My thoughts ramble."

"No, Rifkin," she said, speaking in a tone much like the one she employed with Avarineo. "You did not say you were a common soldier."

"Good," I answered. "I've been a captain of soldiers, among other things."

Annoyed, she said, "You certainly aren't free with tales of your past."

"I'm not proud of my history," I said truthfully. "But I swear on our bond that to the best of my knowledge, I've been nothing and am nothing that threatens anyone who lives in this castle."

After a moment, she nodded. "That's sufficient for me. It may satisfy my brother."

"You speak of him as though he rules you."

"He's lord here. He's older than I am."

"Oh."

"And I'm quite fond of him!" she snapped.

"Of course."

"Are you trying to set me against him?"

"Why should I? I don't even know him."

"Perhaps I am too trusting," she said, then raised one eyebrow. "Why did you choose to take this road in winter?"

"It's spring," I said.

"Only by the calendar. The locals know another spell of cold weather will follow soon. Why did you decide to cross these hills, by this route?"

I shrugged, a gesture that usually served me well. "To reach the far side?"

"That's all?"

"It's purpose enough for me," I said.

"Have you ever heard of Duke Komaki?"

"No."

"Did you know my family ruled these woods?"

"No."

"Or even that witchfolk had a keep here?"

"No."

"You asked no one about the route before you?"

"An innkeeper some two days back told me I'd find no one until I reached the other side of this valley."

"He was either unusually ignorant or he thought to have fun with a foreigner."

"Perhaps."

"My brother may think you're a spy."

"Is this a game? Your brother may think I'm a prince of Undersea. And so long as he doesn't close me in a well, he's welcome to do so."

She reached out to touch my lips with the ends of her fingers and said, "This is for your sake, Rifkin. If you wish to survive here, you'll answer my brother to his satisfaction. If he's not happy to have you as a soldier, he'll find another use for you."

"What use?"

She shook her head. "We live a harsh life here, my Rifkin. If you can fit in, you'll do well. But you must fit in."

"You continue to speak of my satisfying your brother. I did not swear to him."

"It's in my best interest if you serve him as you would serve me."

Two soldiers in bronze breastplates guarded the main gate. An oil lantern at their feet showed that one was a nervous boy. The other, a scarred, broken-nosed woman who wore her grey hair back from her forehead to display a witch's peak, said, "Greetings, Lady." She glanced at me and asked Naiji, "Good hunting?"

Naiji nodded. "I think so. Are the others still out?"

"No. Your brother returned last, perhaps an hour ago. He'll be worried about you."

"He always is. No matter. Watch well, Captain."

"As ever, Lady."

The walls of Castle Gromandiel were in poor repair. I noted a few wide cracks, and not far from the guards' post, weeds so thick someone might climb them, if determined and lucky. But the portcullis rose silently when the second guard let us in. The courtyard was overgrown with grass and a few bushes that threatened to become trees. I asked, "How many soldiers do you keep here?"

Naiji smiled. "If you're a spy, my brother will have to admit you're not a subtle one. We have nine soldiers, and another twelve adults who'll fight if they must. And we have our animal protectors, of course."

I stared at her. "That's all?"

"That's enough. It has to be."

Were Naiji and her people no more than a band of robber-witches who lived in this abandoned ruin? Obviously these people had enemies, now my enemies, whom they feared and guarded against. Who were these foes, now my foes, and what were their forces? I ignored these questions and said, "This place must be ancient."

"It was an outpost of the old Empire. My family held it then, as we hold it now."

"I see." I should, perhaps, have considered that. I knew the legends of the Witches' Empire as well as I knew the names

of every woman of my motherline. But the witches' power had
died thirteen hundred years ago, when iron and steel became
common and witches, always hated and feared, were forced in
most lands to live apart from humanfolk. The possibility of
Naiji's nobility deriving from that time had not occurred to me.
I had believed that all symbols of the witches' domination were
destroyed. Now I, in Castle Gromandiel, was surrounded by
them.

"Do other people know you live here?" I asked.

"Some. The Queen recognizes our right to these woods,
perhaps because no one has contested that right, until now."

"Queen?"

"You've been poorly informed, I see."

"There's very little communication over the hills," I said.
"I thought a king still ruled the Kond, in name at least."

"Queen Janiavy has held the throne for eight months now."

"I see. And who wants to take these woods from you?"

"Duke Komaki. His hold lies at the far end of the valley."

"What claim does he have?"

Naiji smiled. "You play the lawyer again? Very well. The
county of Gromandiel has always lain in the duchy of Komaki,
but Komaki has had no power here since the Empire fell. Now
he tries to convince Queen Janiavy to build a new empire, and
that reasserting control over Gromandiel is the logical beginning."

We had entered the main keep by a small side door and then
taken a long hall lit by a few smoky torches. Even in what
little light the torches cast, I could see dust, cobwebs, fading
paint, stained walls, broken wainscoting, and similar signs of
neglect. Most of the rooms that we passed were bare of furniture, and what furniture remained seemed to have been cob-
bled together by poor carpenters. Only a part of my mind noted
the vaulted ceilings and marble pillars of what may once have
been a richer place than the Sea Queen's palace. I mulled over
Naiji's history and said, "I think I understand."

"No, lawyer. It's more complex than you suspect. The Duke
fears witchfolk. He hopes to begin a new war against us. And
if that isn't cause enough for him to want this castle, he resents
my brother as a rival for the position of the Queen's Consort."

"Should he?"

"Of course. My brother is ambitious too."

"I did hear you say nine soldiers?"

"Yes. Ten, if my brother accepts you."

"And what are the Duke's forces?"

"Sixty or seventy fighters owe obedience to him. If he succeeds in convincing the Queen of his cause, he may command four hundred or more."

"And you hope to win, Lady?"

"Hope has nothing to do with need, Rifkin. Do you wish I'd left you to die in the woods?"

"No. I'm an optimist. Perhaps your brother can sway the Queen to his side."

Naiji smiled. "Talivane will try, of course."

"That's your brother?"

"Yes. Count Talivane Gromandiel."

"You don't expect him to succeed?"

"Not in the way you mean. Komaki's too powerful. Janiavy will never consider attacking him. But Talivane may convince her to withhold her aid, and maybe even her sanction."

"I thought northern nobles cared little for royal permission."

"True, but sometimes the Queen's word can sway a decision."

"In which case, the Duke will attack with only three times as many fighters as we have, rather than thirty?"

"True."

I weighed that with what I had heard so far. "In this fortress we might be able to hold them off."

"I'm glad to hear you speak of yourself as a part of us."

I shrugged.

"We haven't the supplies to withstand a long siege," Naiji said. "And there are too few of us to watch day and night from all parts of the ramparts."

"All of your people are witches?"

"Yes. But none of them can use witchsight for more than a few hours without rest. The use of magic is as tiring as any physical activity, Rifkin. Perhaps more tiring."

"Still, it gives us an advantage. I doubt the Duke's warriors will try to scale the cliffs in full armor."

"Probably not."

"Then you can hex them."

"We can try, Rifkin. Magic isn't as easy or as sure as you seem to think. And even the presence of a little iron can deflect a spell."

"Oh. I assume you have no cannon, then?"

"No."

"Nor muskets either?"

"One. No one's tried it to learn whether it still fires."

"I will." It was easy to consider this while I withheld judgment on the truth of Naiji's tale. I'd only seen a witch in expensive clothes, a simple giant, a woman and a boy in ancient armor, and an abandoned castle. Whoever Naiji might be, my word bound me to her, but I was prepared, though not happy, to be bound to a mad witch.

We had climbed several stairs and stalked several halls, and finally came to a door that appeared to be made of cast or plated brass. It shone like a mirror, saying that not all in this castle had been left to the uncaring hands of time. Naiji gestured for silence, then opened the door.

In that instant I believed all she had told me. The room was a library, filled with tomes bound in stamped leather, cloth scrolls tied with ribbons of varying colors, maps heaped atop each other with their calligraphed borders visible, and, lining the walls and leaning against shelves, paintings of rich folk and strange lands. The floor was covered with rugs of intricate weave imported from the south, each worth a fortune there and of incalculable value here. A globe of sorcerous light hung overhead, illuminating everything as clearly as though this were day. There were a thousand items that told me no robber band could have won and kept such treasures. And all were diminished by the man who sat in a plush green chair by the far wall.

He was Naiji's twin, or perhaps a year older than she. He wore a crimson robe embroidered with gold and black thread and trimmed in ermine. On his fingers, rings of silver and gold with inlaid stones of garnet and sapphire and peridot and topaz vied with each other for attention. His hair was longer than Naiji's, and he wore pale moustaches and a goatee; yet, if he shaved, he might double for his sister. When he stood, I saw that he was taller than she, but only by a bit. He eyed us both with more curiosity than surprise, then held out his arms for Naiji.

She ran to embrace him, and they kissed quickly. "You're well?" he asked. His voice was also like hers, seductive and tinged with amusement or mockery.

Naiji laughed. "Of course!" Then, smiling, she glanced at me. "That's Rifkin. I found him in the woods. Will you let him live?"

⫸ 4 ⫷

MY DAUGHTER'S VILLA

FESCHIANI JOINED ME at breakfast. "Morning, Pipa." She gave
me a quick kiss, then sat across the table from me to stare at
me. "What do you think you're doing?"

"Right now?" I asked, setting down a cup of tea. "I'm setting
down a cup of tea."

"No, Pipa. Your story."

"Ah. I'm writing it."

"Oh." She carefully separated a biscuit and applied apple
butter with generous strokes. "An almost-abandoned castle in
the woods. You, wandering, with only a few hints of any reason
why. How do you expect—"

"You've been reading my pages?"

"Don't sound so shocked, Pipa. Odd that those pages should
be left in the library. On the edge of the desk by the north
window. Where I usually sit when I'm in the library."

"I forgot them there."

"Right, Pipa."

There is no greater solace in old age than a considerate

child. "I'm telling the story you asked me to tell."

"I asked you to tell your story. What's there begins in the middle of—"

"That's the way of the Loh hero-songs."

She opened her mouth, then closed it and frowned. I smiled. She is quick, but I am still Rifkin.

"The Loh hero-songs."

"Correct, daughter. Have I never had the feast-singers sing of Difrek dueling the Black Shark, or of Kinti racing Death to win back her love, or of Sentif uniting the island people to rescue his mother from the Witch Lord?"

"Yes, Pipa. And I've always fallen asleep."

I heard enough irritation in her voice that I said, "And I usually fall asleep shortly after you do. Still, all the hero-songs share one trait."

"Yes. They're incredibly boring."

"Daughter!"

"Forgive me, Father. I stated the obvious before seeing the underlying truth."

I nodded. "Good."

"They're all completely incomprehensible to sane beings."

"Feschiani . . ." I said slowly.

She laughed. "I'm sorry, Pipa. What trait do your beloved Loh hero-songs share?"

"They begin in the middle of the story, when exciting events occur. The earlier parts are revealed in the telling."

"Father . . ." she said, in tones much like mine a moment before.

"Yes?"

"You're not writing a song."

"Well, my sense of scansion isn't very good."

"And you're not writing in Loh."

"Um, I can't. We don't have an alphabet, only symbols. And I've forgotten most of the few I ever learned."

"And it's rather presumptuous to think of yourself as a hero."

"I don't," I said.

"Oh?"

"Not always."

She laughed and came around the table to kiss me. "I think you're a hero, Pipa."

"And I think you want something from me."

"I do. I want to know what happened before you came to Castle Gromandiel."

"I've told you."

"It's not written down."

"Because it's not important. The entire story is in the tale I'm writing."

"Pipa, brace up. It's not."

"You can't know until it's done."

"True. But I want to know about you, Pipa. Your childhood and—"

"Learning about love and sex and death? Those things?"

"Yes."

"It's boring. Every ambitious young twit who claims the name of poet will—"

"It's not boring, Pipa. Please. The stories are connected, you know."

"I'll tell as much as I damn well—"

I saw the next part coming as she smiled gently and I almost said it with her. "Please, Pipa? For me?"

So I will write two stories, I see. I will tell of the Gromandiels, and I will tell of my past. The story of my past is for Feschiani, but the story of the Gromandiels is for me. And if I am lucky, late at night when the sea has been generous and people sit to be entertained by ancient doings, when children listen at the feast fire with their eyes and their mouths open wide to better hear the song, a singer will begin by saying, "This is the story of Rifkin Outcast and the last master of Castle Gromandiel, as Rifkin wrote it many years later in his daughter's villa by the sea."

But perhaps if I am even luckier, a child or two will sit up in bed someday and my daughter will say, "This is a story of your Great-pipa, when he was no older than you, and much sillier."

5

LOH

I DO NOT know what story Farek sang that night. I remember that something wondrous happened, but whether she made me see a single paddler in a small boat riding a God-wave or a swimmer who plucked pearls from the mistresses of Undersea or something far stranger or far subtler than those things, I cannot remember. Farek stopped in the middle of a sentence. She looked around the feast fire at us all with an expression of surprise, and then she fell forward onto the sands.

One of my sisters glanced at me to see if I understood. My brother only continued to dig in the damp beach sand. I stared, for this had never happened. Stories came to an end; it was one of the few rules that I had grasped then, when I was in my third or fourth summer. I did not understand that Farek was very old. The story she was telling would never be finished, for her own story, the story of Farek, ended then. For a feast-singer, it was a good end.

An old man began to wail, even before someone turned Farek onto her back. Someone else said, "She walks with the

29

White Lady," and I turned and ran into the night. Others of
the village cried now, children as well. I raced down the beach
to escape them. Mima had told me of the White Lady and how
She waited for careless children who played with the cooking
fire or drank from Mima's jar of happiness milk when no one
was about. I had not done either, but neither had Farek.

Something had caught me on the beach and swung me into the
air. I hit at it, but it held me firmly beneath my arms. I kicked,
and I thought I screamed, but later I was told I had been
perfectly silent. At least I realized this was not the White Lady
come for me, too. This was a person, and this person laughed.
That made me angry, and I struggled harder. I cursed like my
mother did when she had drunk several jars of the happiness
milk. "Fool sailor! Stupid sea-lover! Let me go, you damned
tide-given witch thing!"

"Shush, little one," the other said in a foreign accent.

"Not little! Not shush! Let me go!" My arms and legs flurried
even more furiously, and then I stopped, suddenly crying with
all my heart. Farek had told stories to me, and sometimes given
me bits of coconut.

The other drew me closer, as if to embrace me, and I kicked
then. "Aiii!" the other screamed, and almost let me go. I wrig-
gled frantically. Then the stranger said, quietly, very calmly,
and without a hint of threat, "Stop."

I only knew that some large and unknown being held me
in the dark, yet the single word uttered so patiently made me
forget about Farek and the White Lady. I forgot that I was
afraid, for I was not used to patience from those I had hurt,
and the stranger's reaction intrigued me. My sisters would have
hit me. My brother would have cried until someone else hit
me. My mother would have hit me, then sobbed and hugged
me and told me she was sorry I was so bad.

"You're all right now?" the other said.

I nodded, which the stranger must not have seen in the dark,
for I was then shaken vigorously. "Yes!" I shouted.

"At least your lungs are fine, little one," he said, setting
me down on the beach.

"Not lit—"

"I'm sorry. What is your name, child of the Loh?"

"Rif."

"Don't be sullen, Rif. Perhaps I did wrong to impede your

flight. If so, I am sorry. I am Tchanin Freefarer, originally from Rassoe."

I giggled at that. The older boys had told a joke that I had not understood, but thought funny: What is the difference between the Sea Queen's palace and a girl from Rassoe? Not everyone has been in the Sea Queen's palace.

"Ah, we are friends now? Good. What is that commotion I hear?"

"White Lady came. For Farek." I sniffled, and wiped my nose on the back of my arm.

"I am sorry, Rif. She was dear to you?"

"Yes. Mima's mima." Then I began crying again, not so loudly as before. I remember being embarrassed that I couldn't stop. Pipa would not have cried. Perhaps I lunged toward Tchanin for an embrace. Tchanin placed a hand against my chest to slow me, then seemed to understand and hugged me. Tchanin's voice had been pitched such that the stranger might have been male or female. The hug let me know he was a man by the feel of his beard next to my head as he patted my back. In a way, that was worse than if he had not tried to comfort me. I had not been hugged by a man since Pipa sailed. I pushed him back.

He accepted this. "Better now?"

"Yes," I lied.

"Good."

We stood there listening to the wind and the sounds of the people by the feast fire. The flame beckoned me. Perhaps Mima had missed me. I was sorry I'd run off, but I was not sure how to return. I felt responsibility for Tchanin, and annoyance at that responsibility. I think I wished he would leave, and then I could sneak into the hut of a large family and sleep.

"Come, Rif." He took my hand and led me toward the feast fire. The people still keened Farek's farewell. She lay on her back on a black robe, a robe I later learned was called the White Lady's robe, which was draped over a yellow boat. The next morning her body would be gone, and we would all pretend she had sailed the boat away. In truth, someone would bury her, and the boat would be repainted and renamed. Loh was too poor to sacrifice a boat whenever a villager died.

The dogs began to bark before we were near the fire. Our Chief, a woman named Sanleel, called, "Who comes?"

Tchanin squeezed my hand, so I yelled "Rif!"

"And a friend," Tchanin said. His voice was loud enough to carry, yet he did not shout.

The people had ceased the lament before Sanleel addressed us. When we stepped within the light of the feast fire, several of the more timid of the Loh scurried away from us in fear or awe. I was immediately proud of my friendship with Tchanin, and I glanced up to see if he was the Sea Queen's consort, or perhaps a demon from Undersea. I knew from my people's reaction that he was more than a man from Rassoe.

He disappointed me. I cannot say what I noticed first, perhaps that he was old. His hair and his beard were streaked with grey, the color of sand on a rainy day. Now that we were near adults, I saw that he was short, shorter than most of the men and some of the women of Loh. His clothes were dyed black, which I had never seen used for clothing, but they were only loose cotton pants and a shirt like most of our villagers wore, and his hemp sandals might have been made by the village ropemaker.

Sanleel nodded to him and said, "Priest," and I turned back to stare at him. That explained the people's reaction, for the feast-singers loved to tell us of the followers of the Warrior-Saint. Those followers could slay thirty warriors as quickly as an eye blinks. Unarmed and without iron or steel, one was the equal of ten witches. A Priest could swim among a pack of sharks for pleasure, or call a whale to beach itself so a village would not starve. Some said Priests could fly, and others that they could not, though they could leap so far that birds became envious and walked henceforth in shame.

That Tchanin was a Priest only confused me. I had thought Priests were taller than palm trees, that their clothes were made of woven moonlight.

Tchanin nodded as deeply to Sanleel as she had to him. "Sanleel Lohchief?"

"Yes."

"I learned your name in Rassoe. I am Tchanin Townbound. I was sent here from the White Mountain."

Sanleel looked at Farek's body, then back at Tchanin. "Departure and arrival in the same evening. It is unusual."

"Yes. I am sorry to come at such a time. Farek Lohsinger's

fame was known on the White Mountain. I had hoped to hear her."

My mother had been in a crowd of children and parents, but she stepped forward then to say, "I am her daughter. Hear me." She wore the tan pants and shirt of our people, and twin braids on one side of her head told that her lover was away. Her voice was thick from happiness milk or grief. I thought I had never seen her more beautiful, or more fearsome.

Another woman, one of her friends, reached for Mima's arm to restrain her. Mima snapped her wrist free. "I am Jisan, child of Farek! Hear me!" She began Kinti's Lament, and even I could tell that her voice was very bad. The other villagers joined in the song after a few minutes, and then Tchanin added his voice, and we sang late into the night.

Tchanin built a hut near the beach, on a bluff not far from our village. Many of our people offered to help him, but he only accepted aid to raise a high center pole, five wall poles, and the radiating beams for his roof. The adults seemed to understand his desire to work by himself. Perhaps they were grateful that he did not demand that the Lohfolk build him a palace. The children were fascinated with this strange little man who talked oddly and lived alone, and since he did not chase us away, we played near his home whenever we could during his first days in Loh.

For the most part, he ignored us. I and a few others helped at times, though I'm not sure now that we helped at all. We gathered rushes and pulled weeds and used sticks to turn a patch of ground for a garden. We turned twice as much ground as he later planted. He never laughed at us to say that we had been overzealous or that he had been clever in keeping us from underfoot.

Most of the children soon tired of Tchanin, for he ignored our pranks and thanked us for our help with a simple nod, and sometimes, a softly voiced "Good enough." After a few weeks had passed, only four of us still went to visit the Priest. I went because I had found him first and therefore thought I had a claim to him. Bellis went, I think now, because she thought the Priest was attractive, not so much for himself as for the awe in which he was held. Svanik went because the Priest did not send him away, as most Loh did. And Vayil went because she wanted to become a Priest someday.

And since I know that Feschiani will ask who these children were, I will write of them now. Bellis was my oldest sister, and her body had already begun the woman's quest to align with the moon. Svanik was the crippled boy, who fell or was thrown into a fire shortly before I was born. Half of his face was scarred and stretched unnaturally, so at times he drooled when he talked. His every expression was a grimace. Vayil was an older girl, the firstborn of the Search line, whom everyone loved because she was attractive and well-spoken.

Feschiani will say that is not enough. Well, Bellis was sterner to me than my mother and not half so demonstrative in her affections. Svanik hit all the younger children when he could, and we called him Coconut Face when we could, and I am not sure who began this pattern. Vayil rarely noticed me, since I was young, but I had watched her play spearball and wished that when I was older, I would play as well as she.

Loh's woodworker brought planks to Tchanin so he could have a floor. He had already made a roof of lashed fronds and constructed frames of bamboo for three of his five walls. He worked the wood floor with a sanding stone that the woodworker had lent him, and after some time, Vayil, Bellis, Svanik, and I helped while he watched.

I should not suggest that we were a band. Bellis was too old to be friendly with Svanik or me, and so was Vayil. Bellis and Vayil had fought over something, I no longer remember what, and so they did not speak to each other. Sometimes one would look at the other when she was looking away. Whenever the other caught the first looking at her, she would raise her head haughtily, and on occasion, laugh. When Tchanin gave us a task, Vayil and Bellis rarely worked together. I usually worked with Bellis, because she was my sister. No one liked ugly Svanik, though he would work with whoever accepted him. When we rested in the heat of the day, we rested apart, Svanik under one tree, Vayil under another, Bellis and I under a third.

During one resting period Tchanin said, "Well, then. You come when I do not invite you, and you work when I ask you, and you come again knowing that I will give you more work. I think you are all fools."

Bellis flushed at that, but Vayil laughed. Svanik's grimace, like most of his expressions, might have meant anything. I laughed because Vayil did, and because Bellis was embarrassed.

"If you will not stay away when you are not asked to come," Tchanin said, with a slight smile beginning to lift the ends of his grey moustache, "then I will ask you to come tomorrow morning at dawn. Perhaps the invitation will keep you away."

It did not. Bellis and I arrived before dawn, but Svanik was already there. Perhaps he had slept in the woods nearby. I knew that he often slept outside his family's hut. His brothers and sisters were among those who called him Coconut Face.

Tchanin was not in the hut. There was enough light for us to see his mat and the small bundle of things he had brought from the White Mountain. We did not enter, though we would not have stayed out of another family's hut, especially one with two walls open to the weather. But one of Farek's best songs had been about a Priest who could kill by setting Death on to any object, and Death would take the next person who touched the thing. Tchanin had said that none of us should touch his possessions. None of us did.

Vayil came running into Tchanin's yard just as the sun began to rise. "Where's Tchanin Priest?" she gasped.

"Here," said Tchanin coming from the beach. His hair and his beard were wet from bathing, and in his black clothes and in the early light, he looked like a visitor from Undersea.

"Gather around," he said, and we came close to him, still standing apart from each other.

"Closer," he said, beckoning with both hands. Reluctantly, we stood beside each other. "I have watched each of you these last weeks. Do you all want to study with me?"

We each said we did with words or nods.

"Then I will teach you, if you are willing to learn. But learning is always painful, and the least pains are physical. Do you understand what I mean?"

Vayil turned her head to one side to question Tchanin, but Svanik brought his hand to his scars and nodded slightly.

Tchanin smiled at him. "I thought you would, Coconut Face."

Svanik glared at the Priest. I laughed and said, "Coconut Face!" Bellis nudged me to be quiet, so I repeated it louder,

"Coconut Face!" Svanik turned from Tchanin to me and hit me below my eye. I fell down, more surprised than hurt, but when I understood what had happened, I yelled in pain so someone would hit Svanik. Tchanin looked at me and said, "No one loves you, Rif. No one."

I don't know if Bellis would have said something, for Tchanin immediately turned to say "And no one desires you, Bellis, and no one ever will." Vayil clenched her fists then, and Tchanin laughed at her. "You would oppose me? You? You'll never amount to anything, Vayil. You'll disgrace your entire family."

"You eat shark guts!" Svanik said. He never mumbled when he was angry. He threw himself at the Priest to hit at his stomach, but Tchanin caught him with an outstretched arm and continued to laugh mockingly. "Coconut Face. Melt Face. Sucker Fish Face."

"Stop that!" Bellis yelled. "Stop that now!"

"Or what?" Tchanin asked. "Perhaps if I desired you, I might listen to you. Who'd desire you?" He glanced at Vayil. "Do you like watching this, coward? You've fooled everyone into thinking—"

"Shut up!" Vayil cried, rushing at Tchanin.

"—you'll amount to something." Tchanin pushed Svanik into Vayil, and they both stumbled to the ground. "You never will."

Tchanin looked at me. "And what about you, Rif? Does it bother you that no one loves you?"

"No!" I brought both arms up suddenly, flinging sand at his face. He covered his eyes with his sleeve and laughed again, but there was something different to this laugh, something less malicious. As Tchanin brought up his arm, Vayil and Bellis and Svanik threw themselves at him together, knocking him back onto the ground and scrambling to get atop him and hit him. He rolled away from them with surprising ease. Standing before they could reach him, he immediately brought the palms of his hands together and bowed to us. He gave us all a gentle smile. "Your first lesson is over. Come back when you wish."

"You stink!" Svanik said.

Tchanin nodded. "Yes. Go, now."

"No one wants you!" Bellis cried.

"Certainly not."

"Come on," Vayil said. "Let's go."

"Yes," said Bellis. She and Svanik turned and followed Vayil out of the clearing. I stared at Tchanin and at the departing children. When he said nothing more, I left too.

I stayed away from Tchanin's hut for several days. At last, I had to know what he had meant for us to learn, and so I went.

When I arrived, he was in the clearing before his hut, showing Svanik how to do the snapping front kick. Tchanin looked over at me and said, "Ah, Rif. Come. Svanik needs a partner." I started to speak, then hesitated and took my place in front of Svanik. Tchanin showed me the block to use for blows aimed below the waist. We took turns, kicking and blocking each other. After a bit I began to smile at Svanik when one of his kicks almost struck me, and I learned to recognize the grimace that he meant as a smile.

Tchanin clapped his hands to signal an end to the practice. He had us bow to each other and to him. When he turned to go into his hut, I said, "Priest, I—"

"Address me as Master," he said quietly.

"Master. Why were you mean?"

He glanced up, then back at me.

"Please," I said. "Why?"

"I said I would be. I'll be meaner yet, if you continue to study with me."

"Vayil thinks you did it so we would all become friends. Because we fought you together."

"Ah."

"Bellis thinks you're mean."

"And what do you think, Rif?"

"I don't know."

"But you've been thinking about this?"

I nodded.

"Then you must have an opinion."

"I think you're a greater fighter than Difrek Sharkslayer."

He smiled. "I think you're wrong."

"I think you should have told us why."

"Why, Rif?"

"To help us learn."

"And why should I help you learn anything?"

I squinted as I thought, and finally said, "I thought you wanted . . ."

"Yes?"

"I don't know. I thought you wanted to teach us . . ." I shrugged, unable to finish the thought.

"No, Rif." He looked out at the beach, and then he smiled. Beckoning to Svanik, he said, "Tell Rif what you thought."

Svanik stared at his feet. "That we're stronger. When we're together."

"Why didn't you say so!" I yelled at Tchanik.

"Calm yourself, Rif. Never shout when you can speak softly. It is more polite and more efficient."

"So?" I screamed.

"And if you shout at me again, I will hit you."

"Oh," I said quietly.

Tchanin laughed. "Rif, I may never explain myself again. I should not explain myself now, but you are young, and I am not proud of my first lesson. Listen, then. Anything I tell you, you will hear, and you may then forget. What I make you discover for yourself, you will remember."

"Why's it important?" I asked.

"For now, it's not. But the Art is always more than it seems to be, Rif. I would not say that if I did not know you are too young to understand it."

6

CASTLE GROMANDIEL

TALIVANE GROMANDIEL PLACED the tips of his ringed fingers together and said, "A good question, my sister. Do you think I should let this Rifkin live?"

Naiji winked at me as she answered. "Oh, do! He has talents."

"Hardly like ours. I could sense his iron before you opened the door."

"Rifkin's a fighter. I saw him kill Avo."

He stared at her and said slowly, "You didn't stop him?"

She looked down to avoid his gaze. "I thought Avo could handle him. I mean, one man, alone..." She glanced back at Talivane. "But you should have seen him! He could defeat two like Avo!"

I said, "Don't feel obliged to test that."

"Indeed?" he said to Naiji, then turned to me. "Come closer." I walked halfway across the room, and the globe of light dimmed. Talivane winced. "That's close enough. Perhaps we should have candles." He lit several by nodding at them, and the illuminating sphere shrunk and disappeared. Talivane sighed. "If we keep you, all your steel will be a constant nuisance."

"Perhaps," I said.

"Where are you from?"

"The Ladizhar," I answered.

"The isles?"

"No. The coast."

"Hmm. And why do you travel north?"

"Wanderlust."

"That's all?"

I dismissed the matter with a tossing gesture. "I haven't a home to hold me anywhere."

"Tell me more, southerner. I can kill you with a lightning bolt, if I decide you're too dangerous to keep. Or too boring."

I set my hand on the pommel of my short sword as though I rested it there. Count Gromandiel laughed. "You think steel will help you? It may disperse most spells, but I've learned that it only attracts lightning."

Naiji nodded when I frowned. "That's true, Rifkin. Had the more powerful of our people known that earlier, the old Empire might still stand."

This interested me. If the Gromandiels were right about the existence of one exception to the laws of iron and magic, there might be others. I asked, "Can you use your lightning against the Duke's soldiers?"

Talivane glanced at Naiji. "Did you tell—"

She nodded. "If he's a spy, he knows already."

The Count said to me, "Yes, southerner. We'll use lightning against your master's forces. But you won't live to tell him that."

"If I have a master," I said, "it's your sister."

"What's this?" Surprise seemed to make him quieter and more cautious. He glanced from me to Naiji.

She put her palm against his cheek. "True. Rifkin swore to serve me."

"Why?"

She spoke dismissingly. "Avo had wounded him. I healed him. I thought he might prove useful."

Talivane stroked his beard as he watched me. "So you're our man, eh, southerner?"

"No," I said. "I'm hers."

He sighed and looked away. "Perhaps I should kill him," he told Naiji. "It would be safer. And far, far simpler."

"No, dear brother. Rifkin may have a lawyer's obsession with details, but he's honest."

His eyes, green but flecked with more grey than hers, flicked back to me. "Will you fight to protect my sister and her property?"

I nodded. "If that's the only way to protect her."

"Her enemies are your enemies?"

"Yes. Just as mine are hers."

"Excellent." He snapped his fingers and the curtains at one end of the room drew themselves back. A man and a woman, both young and blond and dressed all in black, were tied on the floor in the far alcove.

Naiji clapped her hand to her mouth. "No!"

Gags prevented the prisoners from speaking, but their eyes glared in fear or anger. I recognized them for what they were, and wondered why they had come to Castle Gromandiel, and whom they sought.

"Visitors," said Talivane with theatrical pleasure. "From the Duke."

Naiji said coldly, "He hires Spirits, now. What next?"

Her brother shrugged and quoted, "All's fair in war with witches."

The prisoners' clothing was that of Moon Isle's assassins, who called themselves by many names: the Spirits of Death, the Spirits of Freedom... If, as it is said, the Spirits began as a force to overthrow the Witches' Empire, it was logical that they should be employed by the Gromandiels' foe. I hoped that Duke Komaki had only hired a few, that there was no pact between him and the Spirits' entire clan. If such a pact existed, we might as well slay ourselves now. No one could protect Naiji from a thousand silent killers.

"What happened?" Naiji asked.

Talivane pursed his lips, then said, "I was here, studying. Somehow, the Spirits slipped past Avarineo and the others." He glanced at me and smiled. "Most witches can't tell when iron is near. I can sense it around me, almost smell it. It gives me headaches. Though the Spirits only carried small steel daggers, that alerted me. There were seven of them, so I hid myself in a darkness spell until my captain and her guards arrived.

We killed one Spirit. The rest are in the dungeons."

"What do you want with these two?" I asked.

"Knowledge, originally, but they guard their thoughts well. Now I've a second use for them. Prove your loyalty, southerner."

I suspected his meaning, but I said, "How?"

"Kill them."

"They're no threat, so long as they're bound."

"They're a threat so long as they live." He looked at Naiji and then away, and his voice was sad. "My sister is their second target, after me. I learned that much from them."

Naiji's nostrils flared, but she said nothing.

"Kill them, Rifkin," the Count repeated.

I looked at Naiji. She nodded.

"It's not my way," I said. When neither answered, I added, "What would it prove? If I came here to win your confidence, I wouldn't hesitate to kill allies as replaceable as those."

"I didn't ask for a debate," said Talivane. "Only for a deed."

The male assassin writhed against the stone wall, trying to free himself from his bonds. The woman seemed to have fainted, or to be in shock. She sat perfectly still, breathing deeply, with her eyes half-closed.

"My vow—" I said.

"A deed," said the Count. "Now." He raised one pale hand as though he would throw something. I expected to learn then whether lightning was truly his to command.

I stood there, weighing factors. The matter wasn't as simple as slay the Spirits or be slain by Talivane. The assassins' vow demanded that they keep trying to kill the Gromandiels until success or their own deaths stopped them. Though Talivane and I might disagree on the nature of my bond, my first concern was for Naiji's safety. Yet she was safe while the killers were trapped. Talivane had alluded to dungeons where the rest of the Spirits were held. These two could be interred there. That might not ensure Naiji's perfect safety, but nothing could ever do that. Or did Talivane think my vow meant I should also slay the other captured assassins?

My hesitation took all questions of choice from me. The female Spirit, whom I had thought in shock, snapped her bonds in a smooth movement as she rose from the floor.

I had no time to curse myself for failing to recognize what she had done. I knew that certain mystics could tap their bodies' resources at will, and I knew all too well that certain Spirits had similar abilities. Yet I had seen them bound, and had assumed their bonds were sufficient.

The Spirit snatched a wooden stool from the floor and hurled it at Talivane's head. His hand rose to block the stool, which glanced from his arm to his skull. Talivane fell, obviously senseless, into his chair.

The Spirit turned immediately to her companion. His ropes parted before her unnatural strength as though they were made of seaweed. "Slay the Count," she told him in the tongue of Istviar. Her sentence was a barked command so quick and so high-pitched, that it would have been ludicrous at any other time.

The telling takes longer than the deed. My short sword and my dagger were in my hands before I realized why. I wanted to grab Naiji to drag her from the room, but she had snatched up a silver dagger from a writing table and darted between the male Spirit and Talivane.

The male, apparently an apprentice in the assassin's art, was the lesser threat, but to be killed by a student was still to die. Naiji might have a dagger and he nothing, but his movements told me that his studies at Moon Isle had been similar to mine on the White Mountain.

My own reactions told the female Spirit as much about me. She shifted to guard her fellow Spirit. For one moment we formed a tight square before Talivane's armchair. Naiji and the apprentice were farther from the door than the Master Spirit and I, and I could think of no way to distract the Spirits so Naiji could flee. I doubted she would leave her brother, even if a chance arose.

I told the Master Spirit in Kondish, "Go. No alarm will be given."

I sensed Naiji stiffen in surprise at my words, but apparently she gave the apprentice no opportunity to attack her.

The older Spirit said, also in Kondish, "On what promise?" Her voice was still faster than it should be, yet it held no emotion.

"On my word as one who understands the Warrior-Saint's Art."

There was only one thing the Spirit could do. "I accept," she said.

I let my knife drop a fraction, as though I believed her. Her fingers lashed for my throat. I twisted my body and let my knife and sword arms thrust out at right angles to each other, one toward the Spirit and one toward her apprentice.

I was more clever than I was capable. Though my sword caught the apprentice in the chest, my knife passed by the Spirit as though I had aimed at air. Her striking fingers grazed my neck painfully. Her second attack, meant to rip open my chest if I had not turned, paralyzed my left arm. My knife clattered onto the floor.

The apprentice was wounded, but not stopped. I had no idea how to slow the Spirit, so I threw myself against her companion, knocking him down while I kicked to the side with my heel and grunted "Naiji! Run!" The effort made my battered throat hurt worse.

The sole of my boot caught the Spirit's temple. The credit goes to my luck rather than my skill. I was aiming for her ribs while she was ducking to lunge for Talivane or Naiji.

Naiji still tried to keep the apprentice away from her brother. Her silver dagger had been lost in the skirmish. The younger Spirit wielded the knife that had fallen from my numb left hand, but Naiji held the man by his wrists and they wrestled. Though the apprentice was taller than she, I knew something of Naiji's rope-climbing strength. The added factor of the wound I had given her opponent might have let her win, but I dared not leave this to chance. I stabbed the apprentice in the back with my short sword. "Get help!" I shouted as loudly as I could. My voice came out as a croak.

The other Spirit was already standing. Blood trickled from her temple and a bestial snarl came to her face. "If you were not a witch," she told me, "you might have lived. Not now. He was my lover."

"He may still live," I said quickly. "And the woman you wish to slay could heal him. Would you bargain with us for his life?"

Doubt flickered over her face like a cloud across the sun.

"Why hesitate?" I said. "Is the death of a stranger worth more than the life of someone you love?"

I feel sometimes as if my fate is directed by a vindictive god. The Spirit's doubt was sincere, but her apprentice, dying on the floor, gasped "No! Don't let me be remembered as one who shamed us all!"

The Spirit's foot buried itself in my stomach, and I fell, swinging my short sword as I collapsed. The Spirit leaped over it and raced toward Talivane. Naiji's silver dagger hurtled through the air, but the Spirit, only a step from her victim, turned on one heel to dodge it. The blade embedded itself in the oak paneling of the far wall.

Talivane's eyes snapped open at the sound and his mouth curled in a vicious smile. Spirits are trained from infancy to continue any action without faltering, yet I would swear the assassin slowed for the briefest instant on seeing so incongruous an expression on someone who was about to die. Talivane shouted a foreign word and lightning leaped from his cupped hands to bathe the Spirit.

She twitched as if answering to an epileptic puppeteer. The smell of roasting meat came to my nostrils, and my bruised throat constricted to gag my nausea. The woman's skin blackened and cracked under the lightning's blinding glow. An ugly corpse dropped to lie near me.

I scrambled to my feet. Talivane held Naiji with one arm while he peered at the Spirit and then at her apprentice. The man was also dead. "Interesting," said Talivane. "I wonder if he willed his death, or if your sword stroke slew him?"

I could not speak yet, nor did I care to.

"You're all right?" Naiji asked her brother, obviously concerned for him, and at that moment, nothing else.

He nodded.

"I was afraid for you . . ."

He caressed her cheek. "I'm sorry. Forgive me. I thought it . . . necessary."

"Necessary?" I gasped, disbelieving.

He glanced at me, then said calmly, "Yes."

"I'm glad . . ." My breath came slowly.

"Yes?"

"I'm glad I'm not bound to you."

He laughed. "But you are! Obviously my sister's safety is your first concern." He smiled. "And obviously I can protect her better than you. And so, to guard her, you must guard me. Isn't that so?"

I could only cough then, which was probably best.

Naiji stepped away from the Count. "Was this a test?" she asked.

"I didn't plan it, if that's what you want to know."

"You could have ended it sooner."

"Yes," he admitted. "But I watched closely. You wouldn't have been hurt. Not badly, anyway."

She seemed to stifle anger, then said, "What of Rifkin?"

Talivane shrugged. "He proved himself. You certainly may keep him, if you wish."

"I will!" she said.

He laughed. "Ah, Naiji. You think I acted irresponsibly in waiting?"

"Yes."

"No. I would have acted irresponsibly had I accepted Rifkin without testing him. Our people are more important to me than any foreigner, no matter how exotic his appearance."

She snapped, "I didn't—"

"I'm sorry. A jest. I believe you brought Rifkin because you thought he could aid us. Perhaps he can. You'll grant that we learned more about him than he was inclined to tell." He studied me. "What is this 'art' you share with the Spirits?"

I rubbed my throat. "The elder of them had a far greater share than I."

"Speak, Rifkin."

"I do," I said. "Will you ask me to fetch, next? Or roll over and play dead? That'd be easiest, now."

Talivane grinned. "Perhaps we'll paint your face like a jester's, Rifkin. Come, let's seek dinner. Someone else will clean this mess." He held out a ringed hand for Naiji. She nodded and took it, and they went out the door.

I looked at the charred corpse of the Spirit and remembered what skill and dedication had resided there. Then I looked at the pained face of her companion. Whatever else they had been, they had loved each other.

I left the room to follow Naiji. As I walked through the dark and drafty halls, I chanted the death song under my breath for the two Spirits and the bear called Avo. It seemed as if the Black Shark had decided to swim with me this evening. I wondered if he still followed in my wake.

7

CASTLE
GROMANDIEL

IN THE HALL far ahead of me Talivane spoke to someone in a bronze helmet. The soldier saluted with a quick touch of his hand to his forehead and hurried off. The Gromandiels' library would probably be found unsullied when the Count returned to it.

"Come, Rifkin," Talivane said. "Walk with us."

I took a position beside Naiji.

"I'm still curious about the 'art' you mentioned earlier," he said.

Only my annoyance had kept me from answering him before. Truth should never be hoarded. "There's a popular discipline in the cities along the Ladizhar Sea. It translates into your language as, perhaps, the Path, or the Route. Originally it was a means of training the mind and the body through exercise and meditation in order to transcend the world around us."

"An old idea," said Talivane. "I prefer to improve the world."

"A second old idea," said Naiji.

Talivane grimaced in annoyance, but only said to me, "What do assassins and mercenaries have to do with spiritual aspirations?"

"There was one long ago known as the Warrior-Saint. Some say she fell from the Path, some say she strode farthest upon it. Whatever the truth, she took what she had learned in a discipline of denial and used it to build a kingdom."

"This was along the Ladizhar?" Naiji asked.

"Yes," I said. "When the Witches' Empire fell, or so our legends have it. Istviar sprang from the Warrior-Saint's capital."

"Her teachings are still known there?" Talivane said.

"There are many schools, old and new. Each insists it is the only true Path."

Talivane's eyes narrowed. "You've walked this Path?"

"I've tripped over it a few times in my wanderings."

"Will you teach my people what you know?"

"If your sister studies with them, yes."

He nodded. "She will."

"You might ask me," Naiji suggested.

"Will you?" Talivane asked her kindly. "Our people—"

"I might," she answered, turning her head away so quickly that her white hair swirled about her.

Talivane smiled. "Good." He touched a pale strand that rested on her shoulder, then let his hand drop to his side. "I'm not only concerned for our folk, you know. It would be good for you."

"For you too," she said.

He seemed surprised. "Me?"

"The Spirit would have killed you if you'd been alone tonight."

"Maybe." He laughed. "Very well. We'll all become students to your foreign friend."

Light from many candles bathed the hall from the next room. Like the library, it had been kept in a style appropriate to this castle's history, though the decorations were fewer. The oak dining table could have held fifty guests or more in comfort. Portraits lined the wall above the wainscoting. All were of white-haired folk who watched disdainfully from the places where they had posed so many centuries ago.

The woman at the table was darker than most people I had seen since leaving Istviar, though she would have been thought fair among southerners. Her hair was chestnut and her eyes were violet. Her long dress was a vivid red. When we entered, she stood. She was little taller than a child, but her hips and full bosom and delicate features all proclaimed her maturity.

"Ah," said Talivane with a polite nod. "Have you waited long?"

The woman bit her lip, then shook her head.

"Rifkin," he said, "I would have you meet my wife, the Lady Kivakali."

The woman watched the Count with apprehension, yet he hardly seemed aware of her existence. Naiji still clung to her brother's arm as though they were alone in the room. A sandy-haired serving boy at the far doorway watched us all with a carefully guarded mien.

"My lady," I said, bowing with the flourish I had learned when I served in the Sea Queen's guards. A shy smile came to Kivakali's lips, and she nodded to acknowledge me.

Talivane glanced at me out of the corner of his eyes. I could not tell if he thought me mad, strange, presumptuous, or amusing. Naiji's face tightened to restrain a smirk.

"You . . ." Kivakali looked at her husband for approval or permission, then said, "are a noble from some far land?"

"From some far land," I acknowledged. "Hardly a noble, though I thank my lady for her kindness."

Talivane barked a laugh. "You may say *foolishness* if you wish, Rifkin. My wife is hardly the most perceptive of people."

Kivakali blushed and flicked her eyes downward.

"Well!" said Talivane. "I'm hungry. Let's be seated." He strode to the head of the table.

Naiji looked at me to see what I thought of all this. I pretended not to have noticed. She sat beside her brother, opposite Kivakali, and I, wishing I'd had an opportunity to wash, joined her. We made an odd foursome, Talivane and Kivakali in their finery, Naiji in her dirty hunting garb, and I in my torn and bloodstained traveling dress.

Talivane clapped his hands once. The serving boy hurried over with a tray of porcelain bowls filled with curried lentil soup. I waited a minute for a spoon which did not come, then followed my companions' example and drank from the bowl. The boy brought two loaves of black bread and a chunk of goat's cheese. A pitcher of bitter yellow wine followed.

The dinner, though simple, was excellent. The company was not. Naiji chatted of things she had seen in the woods, animals that were out earlier than their wont and plants that grew in formations they had never taken before. Talivane nodded and smiled and acknowledged her every observation without committing himself to an interpretation. Kivakali sat quietly, shoulders slightly slumped, as if to hide herself, only to earn a "Sit as becomes a Gromandiel!" from her husband. She ate little.

"The food's good," I said during a moment of silence.

"It's simple," said Talivane, "but it pleases me."

"Can't get supplies up here, hmm?"

Talivane's look suggested I would take my meals elsewhere, henceforth. Naiji said, "We sent an expedition east recently. They returned with two wounded guards, no gold, and no goods. They said that bandits fell upon them, but the bandits conducted themselves with military precision. As our people fled, they were cursed for being witches and told to leave the lands of the Kond or die, whichever they preferred."

"So leave," I said.

"To go where?" Naiji asked.

"Witchhold," I offered.

"An interesting myth," Talivane said. "But I've found no evidence that such a city exists anywhere outside of children's stories. I'd rather try to create Witchhold here than devote my life to seeking a fable."

I shrugged and returned my attention to my soup, saying, "Never sought, never found."

Talivane slammed his fist on the table. His wife cringed. He said, "I have obligations, foreigner! Would you have my people wander the world, hated and hounded by all they meet?"

"Did I say they should?"

He stared at me, then said, "If you're suggesting I'm afraid to set out—"

"I say what I say, Gromandiel. What you infer is not necessarily what I imply."

He laughed suddenly. "I like you, Rifkin. You've got the stupid courage of a good hound."

"Woof, woof," I said. Naiji smiled and Kivakali put her hand over her mouth to cover a giggle. When I am charming, I am very charming.

Talivane shook his head. "I've sought Witchhold. In person and in print. All I find are references to a land where human and beast are equals."

Kivakali, musing, whispered, "Go east of dawn and west of night, where high is low and dim is bright, and there the dreams of free folk are, where cold is warm, where near is far."

With thick sarcasm, Talivane said, "Thank you, my wife."

Embarrassed, she said, "I heard the song as a child."

"Which tells me nothing, as that could mean twenty years ago or this afternoon."

Naiji said, "My heart, you needn't—"

"I married her," Talivane said. "Do I not endure her wonderfully well?"

Naiji pursed her lips. Kivakali's chin was tucked and her small hands, holding a napkin, trembled.

I told Talivane, "I imagine it's that quality of quiet forbearance that endears you to everyone you meet."

"Don't test my patience," Talivane said. "You've seen my power."

"I'm not your pet, Gromandiel. If you want me to teach your people, fight your foes, or be anything more than your sister's guard, remember that."

He shook his head and smiled. "You speak bravely, Rifkin, yet you sold yourself to Naiji in order to live as her dog."

"She offered a service and told me its price. I accepted."

"Oh?" He cupped his hand in a way that I disliked. "I, then, offer your life to you, if you'll swear to serve me."

"No."

His eyes narrowed. "You would die?"

"I assume you refer to something quicker than old age?"

"I do, Rifkin."

"So you say. I won't believe it until I experience it, of course. I doubt I'd be able to believe it then."

Small sparks began to dance in his palm. "You have two choices. Make one."

"No."

"You doubt I would kill you?"

"I think if you intended to, you would've already tried."

Talivane nodded, and the sparks disappeared. "You're right."

"Then play no more games with me," I said, wondering if

anyone else noticed that the smell of fresh sweat had joined the odors of my jacket.

"You order me?" He seemed more incredulous than affronted.

"I advise you."

"A fine distinction."

I sighed. "You've been trying to learn about me with your little tests, witch lord. You think that understanding me will give you power over me. I'll offer you understanding, then, and you may take it as power, if you can. Along the coast of the Ladizhar those who try to take another's life forfeit all right to their own. If I ever believe you are sincere in any threat made against your sister or me, I'll kill you and think no more about it."

"A bold statement, Rifkin."

"You wouldn't say that if you knew me, Gromandiel. I'm not fond of death." I sipped my wine. "I'll offer another bit of knowledge to you, the First Step of the Path: The reason for the world is life, and the reason for life is the world."

"Typical circuitous mysticism."

"That's because you hear my words, but not what they imply. If life is the purpose of the universe, premature death is heresy. For me to tell you that I would kill—"

"But you have killed," Naiji noted.

"Only those who attempted to kill others. Were I wiser, I might've found a better way to escape the bear and avert the Spirits."

Talivane turned to his sister and sadly shook his head. "This is the fighter you bring me?"

"If he can stop Komaki without killing, I, at least, would be content, dear brother. And if he can't..." Naiji smiled at me. "Then our pacifist will have to slay as many of the Duke's warriors as the most kill-mad of our band."

Talivane patted his lips with his napkin. "Our conversation takes a rather morbid turn."

"It's not as if we're sure Komaki will attack," Naiji told me. "We only suspect it. My brother sent a message by pigeon to Queen Janiavy just yesterday, asking her to sustain the peace."

"It didn't arrive," said Kivakali.

Talivane stared at her.

"The cook dreamt of a small bird shot with a green arrow," she explained hesitantly.

"The cook," Talivane said with a sneer.

Naiji laid her hand on his arm. "Dovriex is almost as good a seer as he is a chef."

Talivane still watched his wife. "Green, you said?"

Kivakali nodded.

"Your father's color."

"Yes."

"I never should have married you."

She gnawed her lip. "I . . ."

"Yes?"

"I don't aid him against you."

"Of course not. You're too cowardly for that."

She stood and threw her napkin at him. It fell short of his plate. "I also know my duty!" Her eyes had filled with tears. "I . . ." Her features were etched in anguish as she glanced at each of us. "Please, excuse me," she gasped, then covered her face and ran from the room.

Talivane sighed as he brushed aside Kivakali's napkin. "I might enjoy her outbursts more if they were more original."

"She suffers," I said.

"Who doesn't?"

"In the south, unhappy alliances are easily ended."

"I won't surrender her dowry, Rifkin. Nor will I return Komaki's daughter to him."

Naiji, seeing my expression, said, "The old king forced the marriage on us, partly to prevent war, partly to keep my brother from wooing Janiavy."

I said, "That seems to have proven futile, on both counts."

Naiji nodded. "Komaki seems to think his daughter's safety is a price worth paying. And Kivakali, while she lives, may keep my brother from marrying Janiavy, but she can't stop him from being the Queen's lover."

"You're very free with this information."

Naiji glanced at Talivane, then said, "You'll learn it all if you live with us. Anything I tell now may keep you from acting stupidly in the future."

Talivane nodded. "I've little tolerance for stupidity."

"It must be very difficult, being you."

He closed his eyes and breathed deeply. "I think it would be best if you left us now."

Naiji nodded agreement. She stood and stepped behind her brother's chair to massage his forehead.

"The boy," Talivane said, "will show you to your quarters. Chifeo, take Rifkin to the room that adjoins my sister's."

"Yes, master," the boy whispered.

"See that all his needs are met."

"Yes, master."

"A bath might be a good start."

"Yes, master."

I said, "I don't suppose you have little toy ships or ducks that float in the tub?"

"No, Rifkin."

"Yet you assume all my needs can be met. Ah, well. Lead on, Chifeo."

The boy took me back toward the library. He was quiet, probably overwhelmed by my wit. I was in no mood to talk. I had decided I despised Talivane and pitied Kivakali, though I did not know what to do about either. Naiji confused me, but my relationship with her was already shaped by my vow. It was best not to think about her at all.

The presence of the four captured Spirits in the dungeons disturbed me, as did the possibility that more might come. Or would Komaki give up on assassination and turn to attack? The thought of the Duke made me think again of his daughter, who seemed to deserve better than life had given her. Talivane's opinion of his wife was obvious. I wondered what she thought of him.

"Here, Lord," said the boy, opening a plain wooden door—which was, I realized, a luxury by Castle Gromandiel's standards. Most of the doorways that we had passed had been draped with tapestries or animal skins to replace doors that, I assumed, had rotted away in the centuries since this castle's prime.

"My name is Rifkin," I said.

"Yes, Lord."

"When I was your age, I kept a dog called Lord. I'd prefer you called me Rifkin."

He stifled a grin. "Yes, Lor—"

"Woof," I said.

It worked even better than it had at the dinner table. He laughed.

"Rifkin," I said.

"Rifkin," he agreed.

I stepped into the room. It was small, barely large enough to hold a sleeping pallet, but it was clean. The stone walls were bare, though an old rug, once red, covered most of the floor, and a sea-green quilt looked nice enough to have been Naiji's. An elaborate door, carved with hunting scenes, was set into one wall. "That's to Lady Naiji's quarters?"

"Yes."

I tried the latch. It would not lift. "You have the key?"

The boy shook his head. "Only Lady Naiji."

"No matter. This'll do."

Chifeo nodded. He strode to a blanketed portal at the rear of the room and announced, "The bath."

I looked in. A hot spring had been channeled to flow into a marble basin. The water departed through an enameled brass grill at the far wall. "This isn't used for sewage, is it?"

He looked shocked. "No!" He pointed at a low stone seat covered by a wooden lid. "That's the, ah . . ."

"The ah, eh?" I said. "A useful word to know in any language."

He looked at me from the corners of his eyes.

"You've lived here long?" I asked.

He nodded warily.

"And you're happy here?"

"I'm a witch."

"That means you're happy?"

"Here, yes. I remember Kondia. I'm happy here."

"You fear Count Gromandiel?"

"Of course. He's the mightiest of us all."

"Really?"

Chifeo whispered, "He intends to rebuild the old Empire."

"Oh? He seems to be lacking in resources."

"There are hundreds of witches, maybe thousands, ready to join him!"

I looked around the room, lifted the lid of the toilet, then shrugged. "And well-hidden."

"Most are afraid to come," he said. "We must prove we can stand against Komaki. Then every witch within five hundred miles will join us."

"You seem sure."

He nodded. "Count Gromandiel has never failed."

"It only takes once," I said, "to ruin a perfect record."

Chifeo glared. "You wait. The Count'll succeed!"

"I hope so, lad. Truly. Didn't you hear? I'm bound to his sister."

"Oh. Well, don't worry. We're going to rule the world soon."

"That should be fun," I said.

"I believe someone said you're from the south, Lor— Rifkin?"

"Yes."

"I hear it's better for witches, there."

"No one's trying to exterminate them, anyway."

"I've heard that witches still rule there."

"Not since the Spirits helped overthrow the Seaprince," I said. "Leave me, Chifeo. I'll bathe now."

"But I'm to assist—"

"Strangely, I've managed to wash myself alone in the past. It is a talent of mine."

"Oh."

"And we're more prudish in the south."

"Oh. I'll fetch towels."

"Good."

The moment he was gone, I stripped my tattered clothing from me and hid the hairpin and the stiletto with its thigh sheath in my boots. I found soaps for my body and hair in jars near the basin and was resting in the bath when Chifeo returned.

"May I enter?"

"Of course."

He stepped in, noticed me in the water, and frowned. "I thought you said you were prudish."

"Only about dressing and undressing."

"Southerners are weird."

"That's been said before."

He carried a bundle of clothing and towels. When I saw that he was about to take away my torn apparel, I said, "Leave the boots."

"They're not in very good shape."

"Neither are my wits, yet I'd rather have them than another's."

The boy, unimpressed, shrugged and left. I lay still in the waters for some time and was almost in danger of falling asleep when I heard footsteps behind me.

"Chifeo?" I said.

"Hardly," Naiji replied, "though he could be summoned." She walked in front of me, smiled, and let her robe, a simple thing of blue silk, fall to the floor. "I felt bad that we didn't have any toy ducks to give you company while you washed. Will I do instead?"

I smiled. I was slightly embarrassed being naked in front of her without any warning. Her nudity embarrassed me, too, for I did not know these people's customs. Did she think that a boundman's duties included scrubbing backs in baths? Her body was lean and pale and strong, and I hoped she expected me to be more than a bath attendant. She met my gaze, then blushed and covered her breasts with her arm. I wanted to say something like "I think I'm in love." I only said, "Can you quack?"

She gave a perfect duck call.

"You'll do very well."

She slipped into the other end of the basin. "Know any water games, stranger?"

"One," I said.

"Good."

I squeezed my fist just below the water's surface, squirting her face.

"Hey!"

"My son taught me that one."

She shook her head, spraying water like a dog. "Remind me never to bathe with him." She rose on her knees to dunk me.

"Unlikely," I said. "He's dead."

Her eyes opened wide.

"Apologies," I said. "That wasn't fair of me. It happened years ago. Don't worry about it."

"I'm sorry."

I drew a circle in the air with my finger. "It's the Path."

"For your son," Naiji said. "I'm sorry for you."

"It doesn't bother me anymore . . ."

"That's good."

". . . much."

She touched my cheek, then slid beside me. The sides of the shallow basin were curved so one person could lie sprawled, but two had to cuddle. Very aware of her hip against mine, I said, "It was years ago."

"You don't look any older than I."

"Appearances are deceiving."

She laughed. "You're talking to a witch." She placed a hand on my chest. "This isn't an old man's body."

"Maybe I'm a shape-shifter."

"Maybe," she said. "I see one shape that's beginning to shift."

We kissed then. I can't say who began it. We explored with touch and scent and taste where sight had already been. Sometime later Naiji moved up by me so her face was inches from mine. "I like you," she said thoughtfully, perhaps a little amused. "You are . . . appreciative."

"Very," I agreed. I turned and lifted her from the water to the floor. "And I have a strong sense of fairness."

I slid down, kissing her stomach, then licking her navel, which made her laugh. "Stop that!"

"If you wish." I sat up and reached for my new clothes.

She squinted at me, pursed her lips, and said, "I'd be more convinced if I thought you'd be able to button your pants."

I dropped the clothes there and rolled onto her. "Comfortable?" I asked.

"Anyone ever say you talk too much?"

The floor of a bath is no place for lengthy couplings. Perhaps uncomfortable sites for passion are all the more exciting because they seem so inappropriate. My release came moments before hers. I continued the dance of hips, trusting the little man to stand a short while longer, and that short while was enough for Naiji.

We lay still in shared silence. I wondered what I should say to her and whether I should say anything at all. She seemed to sleep. When her eyes flicked open, she grinned. "A bed next time."

"Now?"

She laughed. "Old man. Right. You look as if you haven't

seen twenty-five winters, and you act as though the count is more like fifteen."

I should have had a retort ready for that, but I didn't. I said, "About this matter of who I am—"

She hugged me. "You're Rifkin. That's enough."

I didn't say anything.

"Isn't it?"

Part of my soul craved the safety of secrecy. Another part said *Speak. What does it matter? The past is a far land, where none return.* Yet I only said "Yes. I suppose so."

8

THE WHITE MOUNTAIN

"THE WITCHES ARE our enemies," Tchanin Priest would say whenever a new student joined us. A few of those later students came from Loh, but most were sent from neighboring communities to live with relatives in our village or to stay in the students' hut that we built during Tchanin's fourth year in Loh. Kiyan of Istviar was the seventeenth student to join us, and she stood at the far end of the students' line. I watched her from my place as Second Student.

I had thought the accents of those from Istviar were amusing, until I heard Kiyan speaking. I had thought the shorter sleeves and pants of the Istviarfolk were the sort of things that fools would wear, until I saw them on Kiyan. I had thought that women should be short and pale and long-haired and small breasted and perhaps ten thousand other things, until Kiyan came to our class.

Kiyan said, "There are many families of witches in Istviar, and—"

"That," said Tchanin, "is the shame of Istviar."

"They've never harmed anyone."

"They've never had the opportunity. You all wear steel or iron jewelry, don't you?"

"Yes, master, but—"

"But you forget why you wear it." He sighed. "It is the way of people. It's why your mother has sent you to study with me, Kiyan. She has not forgotten."

"My mother lives in the past."

Tchanin nodded. "Because she is wise. Listen, Kiyan. You've heard the old songs, yet you haven't learned from them. Why did the Warrior-Saint discover the Art? Because she and her people were slaves to the witches. They were forbidden to have weapons, so they had to learn to make anything a weapon, to make themselves into weapons."

"They forged iron weapons in secret, Master Tchanin."

"Of course. But only later, when the secret of iron had been learned. That was long after the Art had been perfected."

"And they nearly exterminated the witches."

I heard a hint of accusation in Kiyan's voice, but if Priest Tchanin heard it, he ignored it. He said, "It was their only failure, Kiyan. They were tired of killing. And so we exist, to ensure that the witches never rule us again."

"How can they?" She touched her metal necklace.

"They can wait for us to think they are defenseless. So we must be vigilant."

Tchanin had never been so patient with the rest of us, and so we knew that Kiyan's mother was important. But a part of me wondered if it was his way of saying that Kiyan was not wise enough to learn.

"Why don't you murder them all?"

"Because they are not a threat now. We watch them, Kiyan. We will watch them until they threaten humanity. And then, if we act, it will be in humanity's defense. We are not murderers. We are followers of the Warrior-Saint."

His voice said he was done, and Kiyan heard that, for she bowed to him. Svanik, standing beside me in the Third's place, gave the grimace that meant he was amused: silly foreigner needed to hear what everyone knew. Vayil, in the First's place, continued to watch Priest Tchanin without letting any of us know what she thought.

After a session of free sparring, Tchanin had us form two

lines. We would practice combinations of moves with a partner, so I watched the lines. When I saw where Kiyan would be, I let a younger student stand on my left rather than my right, so I would be Kiyan's partner.

She had studied somewhere, and she would not stay in the least place in our class for long. Between moves I whispered, "Who taught you? Your mother?"

"No. I stayed a year on the White Mountain."

"Oh," I whispered, as though I did not care, but I was impressed. Tchanin had told us that we would not go to the White Mountain until we were ready to take the Master's Test. I had not known anyone else could go.

"They thought I was weak."

"Your form's good."

"About witches."

"Ah." I looked for Tchanin and saw that he was still far from us. "There aren't any around here. My mother pities them. She thinks they took advantage of power because they had the opportunity to do so. She thinks anyone would, and we should forgive them. It's been centuries, after all."

"Your mother sounds wiser than these fools."

I nodded and didn't tell her that Svanik and I had been telling witch jokes just that morning.

I tested to become a Priest in my seventeenth year, and that meant nine months of training in the Wooden Temple atop White Mountain. Most of us were sad to leave our families in Loh. Vayil almost stayed behind, for her family said she was an adult and must forget the Priesthood to learn the trade of the Searich clan. She came anyway. I said farewell to Bellis, who had become head of our family after Mima drowned, and to the rest of my family in Loh, and the parting was tearless. I saved my tears for my parting with Kiyan.

We met in a bamboo grove near Tchanin's home. The day was very warm. Kiyan waited for me, wearing only the loose, ankle-length pants that should have made her seem one of us. They were made of a very fine cotton and let all of us know that her family must be important. When I saw her, I said, "H'lo, rich girl."

"You're such a dope, Rifkin." I thought I'd angered her,

but she threw her arms around me. Our embrace might have become something else if she hadn't stepped back. "You're going?"

"Yes."

"I'm not."

"Why?"

"Stupid Priests."

"Yeah." I shrugged in sympathy. When I was with her, I understood her fear and mistrust of the Priests, or thought I did. I also suspected there was a reason she had not told me.

"My mother wants me to come back."

"You and Vayil. Everyone's expected to learn the family business." I laughed. "Envy me, rich girl?"

"Course not. You're a dope. You think I should feel sorry for you because you're a poor dope."

"I'm not poor," I said, repeating Tchanin's thoughts. "I'm free."

"You're a free dope," she said, but she smiled, and I might have challenged the Black Shark then, if it had appeared before us.

"Yeah," I said. "Marry me."

"I can't."

"Your mother's a dope. Everyone's a dope."

"I do love you, Rifkin."

"Yeah. Sure."

"It's just—"

"Yeah."

She glared and said, "Would you come to Istviar if I asked? Would you give up the White Mountain and the name of Rifkin Priest?"

"Would you ask me to?"

"Maybe. That's what you're asking me. To give up Istviar and live with a bunch of Priests. I couldn't live on poor people's handouts, Rifkin."

"We could have a garden. We could fish. We could—"

"Yeah. Sure."

I put my hands on her bare shoulders. "The Priests aren't bad, Kiyan."

"They're capricious. They talk of mastering ways of fighting in order to be confident enough to never have to fight. It's insane, Rifkin. I watch Tchanin, sometimes. He's proud, you know. Proud of what he can do. And he likes to watch us fight."

"You can't judge the philosophy by its followers, Kiyan. Tchanin said that. He knows he's not perfect."

"If you can't judge a philosophy by its followers, how can you judge it?"

We'd had this discussion before. I tried to turn it aside by saying, "What do you think we are, Moon Isle Spirits? They're insane. They pervert the Warrior-Saint's teachings; we don't. The White Mountain disapproves of them. We want to be the best we can be. We want to help the poor, the defenseless—"

"You want to be the hero of a feast-singer's song, Rifkin."

I almost hit her. I said "Sure."

She took my hand and said, "I'm sorry. I didn't mean we should part like this. Rifkin, if you ever come to Istviar, find me."

"Find you? Just ask the first person I meet where Kiyan lives?"

She laughed and nodded.

I realized then that I would never see her again, that our lives had taken very different paths. I laughed with her. "When I come to Istviar, I'll ask for Kiyan."

My nine months on the White Mountain were much like the previous years in Loh, except that our classes lasted all day. We studied in good weather and bad, from early morning to late evening. And one morning I awoke to see Tchanin kneeling beside my sleeping mat with an uncharacteristic smile upon his face.

"Good morning, Rifkin Student. Today, if your spirit proves itself, you will become Rifkin Priest."

I nodded carefully. I had wondered when the time would come and what the test would be. Once, a few years after Tchanin came, I had asked when I would become a Priest of the Warrior-Saint. Tchanin had answered, "When you no longer ask."

I knew nothing of what to expect. Tchanin gave me no clues, so I stood and dressed in my student's pants and shirt, then followed Tchanin into the hall. He paused by the toilet, so I made use of it. He led me to the dining room, where rice and vegetables were being served. I ate sparingly. When I was done, he took me back through the hall to the practice room— a large white-walled room with smooth, teak floors—where we studied and sparred when the weather was very bad and our teachers thought to spare us or themselves from wind or rain or snow.

The six Master Priests sat cross-legged in a black line at the far end of the room. A woman in a student's tan uniform stood facing them, and even from behind I recognized Vayil by her curly hair and her perfect posture. Tchanin gestured for me to stand beside her. He sat with his fellow Master Priests. Priest Binnuth nodded to each of us. "Greetings, students of the Art. A place awaits you among the Priests." My heart leaped with pride. I suspect that Vayil's did too. Binnuth added, "Which of you will take it, and which of you will leave us?"

I swallowed. Vayil had always been First Student. Though I had defeated her in a few practice bouts, my victories had been rare. Binnuth smiled as if she had made a joke and said, "That is what we are here to learn. Sit, now."

We meditated for some time, but my mind would not calm. I thought about becoming a Priest and I wondered what I must do to succeed. Vayil could return to Loh and take her place in the Searich clan. They would be proud to have her back. I would be laughed at for my failure. If I was lucky, one of the fishing families would give me the least place on a boat. And I would take home the least share of the catch. And perhaps I would soon give half of my share for happiness milk, and when I had drunk enough, I would go for a swim like Mima did, late one evening when the sea was still.

When Binnuth clapped her hands, Vayil and I rose. Something in Vayil's face said that she had not quite calmed herself either. I think it was then that I understood how very much she wanted to earn a place of her own, a place that no one could say she had been given because of her family.

We did all of the thirteen traditional patterns together. First Pattern was difficult, even though Tchanin had taught it to me during my first week of instruction in the Art. It consisted of a few of the most basic techniques, but because they were so basic, they should be done perfectly. Because I was not calm, I was too aware of every mistake I made. The Master Priests watched without commenting, without smiling or coughing, and only rarely moving a finger or a chin to indicate to a fellow Priest a move done poorly or well. I could not decipher their gestures, so I ignored them.

"Good," Binnuth said when we finished the Thirteen Patterns together. "Very good. I think that only a bout between you two will decide who succeeds. The usual rule of halting your blows at the point of contact will not apply in this test."

I glanced at Binnuth, not sure that I had heard correctly. She still smiled. Embarrassed at my lack of control, I faced Vayil and bowed. The floor was cold and slick beneath my feet. Vayil's face was as unreadable as mine. We circled each other, each in sparring stance, and I wondered how I could defeat her when she knew every trick I had learned and knew every one better.

She probed my defense with a front kick, which I deflected easily. She skipped in, snapping her closer fist at my chin. As I blocked that, she came in with a blow to my side. I spun, but the blow connected, and hurt. I wondered for an instant if the Priests would stop us. I did not slow myself in the hope that they would.

I continued my spin and came about with a sweeping back kick. Vayil caught my leg and pushed me forward to the floor, pinning me to the ground. She expected the Priests to stop us then, I think, so she didn't follow up with a blow to my kidneys. I rolled free of her. I kicked at her, only thinking to keep her away. The kick caught her chin, and she fell backward.

I glanced again at the Priests, hoping that one of them would speak. They watched. Tchanin was no different, and I wondered what he wanted of me. I glanced back at Vayil in time to see her come for me with a side kick, and I skipped several steps backward to avoid it.

I realized then that I liked Vayil. I had always thought I hated her for being attractive and diligent and wealthy, for being older, for being better at the Art than I. For the year before Kiyan came to Loh, I had desired Vayil, and she had never treated me as anything more or less than a fellow student. Svanik and I had joked about her, but as I saw her standing before me, I knew that I loved her, perhaps more than I loved Kiyan. I also knew that only one of us would leave this room a Priest.

I came in with a flurry of punches to her face, and several

connected. She kicked at me, but I dodged and hit her again, knocking her down. Still the Priests said nothing. Vayil stood, her face bloody and ugly, and came forward. I kicked her in the stomach. She doubled up, spat blood, then stood, raising her fists. I kicked again, a forward sweeping kick, and she dropped to the floor.

"I've won," I said quietly.

"Have you?" said Binnuth, turning to Vayil. "Has he?"

"No," Vayil said, struggling to stand.

I whispered to Vayil, "Don't." She shook her head, and her hair flew about her battered face. I caught her arm as she punched and twisted it behind her back. "Quit!" I whispered.

She stomped my foot as she brought her free elbow back into my chest. Avoiding those blows, I let her loose. She shook her head again and kicked at me. I shoved her hard, knocking her down again.

I don't know how many times we played that scenario. I kept trying to think of techniques to incapacitate her without killing her or breaking bones, but I could not. I wondered if that was what the Priests wanted, for the weaker of us to die. Time after time Vayil stood, Vayil threatened me, and I hit her. It seemed to me that this might be the cruelest fate I could imagine, to be winning forever and never to have won.

When she finally fell and did not rise, I hardly believed it. When I saw that she would not get up, I knelt beside her to be sure that she was breathing freely. I carefully turned her, suspecting this might be a trick on her part, but she was unconscious. I pitied her as she lay there, for I knew that waking to failure would not be easy. I hated myself for having to win. I hated the Priests for making me win. Yet a part of me was very proud; Tchanin's promise that learning would be painful had been too horribly true, yet I had learned and I had won. I stood to face the Priests.

Tchanin was weeping. All of the Priests seemed to be sad or embarrassed or feeling something I could not recognize. I said hesitantly, "I've won."

Tchanin looked away. Rising, Binnuth said, "You may go, Rifkin. We will care for Vayil Priest."

I walked for three weeks from the White Mountain to Istviar, and I lived on charity and petty theft. When I came to the City of Ships, I almost decided to return to Loh. Istviar was larger than I could comprehend. In one minute more people passed me on its streets than inhabited the whole of Loh. Its gaily painted bricks made Loh's weathered wooden huts seem shameful things. I watched the crowd of passing cityfolk for someone with a kind face, and finally I asked a middle-aged woman in patched robes for help. She laughed. I did not know if she laughed at me or at my question. I almost left before she could say, "You seek a slim girl of sixteen years, Kiyan by name, whose mother is important? You must be from Rassoe."

"No," I said. "Loh."

"Ah. Well, boy of Loh, you seek the daughter of the Sea Queen. Ask at the palace, if you wish." She pointed at a tall, graceful building in yellow and gold that overlooked the harbor.

"The daughter of the Sea Queen?"

"Yes."

I realized that this did not surprise me, perhaps because I'd never given a great deal of thought to the Sea Queen's power. I knew Kiyan had secrets from the Lohfolk, and this had been one.

At the palace I asked a servant if Kiyan was busy. The servant blinked, saying, "The Little Queen? I'll ask. And you are . . . ?"

"Rifkin Freeman."

The servant returned smiling, and took me around the palace to a small garden of rocks and ferns and cactuses. Kiyan waited there with several attendants, but she gestured for them to leave as I approached. She wore closely tailored pants and a shirt of gold thread and a black sash, and her hair was longer than when I had seen her last. She looked at my face and said sadly, "Oh, Rifkin. Poor Rifkin."

"You were right," I said. "The Priests are all crazy."

"Shush," she said. No one disturbed us, and we stayed there for the rest of the afternoon.

9

CASTLE GROMANDIEL

I WOKE IN the middle of the night to a scream. It came from far away, and I might have thought it the wind if I had never been to war.

I was alone on my sleeping pallet. Naiji had left me after one last dalliance, saying that though she would lie with a boundman, she would never sleep with one. I snatched up my axe and short sword and dashed nude to the door that connected our rooms. No one answered my poundings. Her door was bolted from within, and I cursed myself for not telling her to leave it unlocked.

I ran into the hall. Neither torches nor candles burned in the wall sconces. A few windows opened on the courtyard, but they were narrow slits from which archers could fire at intruders who had breached the main gates, and most of the windows were hung with rags to reduce drafts. Little light escaped the drapes to help me. My eyes had adjusted enough to see some shadows as darker than others, but nothing more. I found the latch to Naiji's hall door by touch and memory. It did not turn beneath my hand.

"Naiji!" I shouted. Only silence greeted my call.

I kicked to the side, striking the oak planking with the heel and edge of my foot. Shock raced through my entire leg. The door rang like a giant bass drum. It did not give.

I had kicked again and failed again when a dark shape hurried down the hall. "You," the other said. I recognized the voice of Talivane's grey-haired captain and realized that she must be using witchsight. "You might practice your technique when no one sleeps."

I said, "Open this door."

"Why?"

"I heard a scream. It didn't sound like passion."

"It wasn't from Lady Naiji's room."

"No? Where is she?"

"She doesn't answer to you, you know."

"I must know that she's safe."

"Or?"

I could see that the captain's bronze sword was unsheathed. I wondered if she could sustain her witchsight while fencing against my steel weapons. "I must know that she's safe," I repeated.

"Why?"

"It's my job."

The captain sighed. "Come."

We walked down dark halls and I began to wish I had dressed. The soles of my feet cringed with each step, and my shoulders began to shiver. "I don't suppose you'd care to lend me your cloak?" I asked.

"Not really."

"You may have noticed that I'm not wearing any clothes."

"Oh, my," she said. "I'm shocked. Simply shocked." After a moment, she added, "I see it isn't true, what they say about your people."

I decided not to ask whether this was a compliment or an insult.

The only noise was the slight scuffing of Feschian's boots on the dusty floor. When I felt the tiles become slippery clean under my feet, I knew we approached important chambers. The captain stopped me with a firm hand against my chest. She knocked loudly against a door that I could barely see.

Talivane's weary voice answered. "What now?"

"The lady's pet is restless," said the captain.

"Is Lady Naiji safe?" I asked.

"Rifkin," said Naiji from the far side of the door. "I thought you'd be too tired to wake again."

"You're well?" I asked.

"Yes."

"And the scream?"

"That was not me."

I waited a moment, then asked, "And I needn't know who it was?"

"He is quick," said Talivane, loudly enough that I might easily overhear.

"It sounded as if someone died."

"That's correct," said Talivane. "We were questioning one of the Spirits. He was too reluctant to speak."

"I see."

"I'm well," said Naiji. "Go back to sleep, Rifkin."

"Fine," I said as civilly as I could, and I stalked off.

The captain followed.

"You want something?" I asked.

"You're returning to your room?"

"Why do you care?"

"First, it's my job to know where everyone is. Second, your room's back the other way."

"Oh." I turned around and continued walking.

"You seem angry."

"Do I?"

"The Gromandiels are masters here. They act as they please."

"I know that."

"You disapprove of torture? The Spirit, if he had been convinced to speak, might have said something that could save us all."

"Perhaps." I consciously relaxed the tensions in my limbs, for I feared that if I did not, the captain would see that I understood too much: Talivane had lied to me, and not well.

That someone died, I did not doubt. That it was one of the Spirits, I could accept. But torture is a messy business. Talivane, fastidious as he seemed, would hardly have prisoners brought up from the dungeons to bleed and piss and puke and sweat and shit on his bedroom floor. Further, he would never allow anyone to escape him by such an easy path as death.

As for Naiji's presence at whatever had happened, I could only remind myself that her morals were not mine, that our relationship was delineated by the words of our vow. And yet I had to admit that I liked the way she cocked her head to one side when she considered a question, the way she had laughed almost childishly when we were alone in the bath and she had done something that especially pleased me, the way—

"It won't be easy for you," the captain said.

"That's an expression of sympathy?"

"Of some sympathy."

"Which means you'll lend me your cloak?"

"We're almost to your room, southerner."

"Call me Rifkin."

"Call me Lady."

"What a coincidence. I had a dog once named—"

"Or call me Captain, if you prefer, or Feschian."

"Why?"

"That's my name. I wouldn't have you confuse me with a bitch."

"Unlikely. There's only one..."

"What?"

"Nothing." I wouldn't make jokes at Naiji's expense, whether she deserved them or not.

"You should be careful in this castle."

"Really? A shame. I'd planned to spend my time traipsing about, festooning the gargoyles with lily garlands."

"Oh?" said Feschian.

"Maybe not," I conceded. "I doubt Avarineo would wear his."

"You act like one of those youths who consider themselves troublemakers."

"Hardly. I'm one of those old men who consider themselves troublemakers."

"Very funny, Rifkin. Naiji says—"

"Naiji?"

"She's only the Lady Naiji before strangers and those who believe in protocol."

"Like her brother?"

"Like her brother," Feschian agreed.

We stopped in the hall. The captain seemed to be waiting. "You were saying?"

"I was saying that Naiji said you fashion yourself a philosopher."

"Never," said I. "A philosopher is someone trapped in a web of words, lost in a maze of metaphors, buried beneath a..." I searched for a suitable phrase.

"A philosopher," said Feschian, "is someone who blames his inability to perceive the universe on the universe itself, or on the nature of perception. You're not that."

"Good."

"You're just someone who hasn't decided whether he wants to die. Don't endanger Naiji if you choose death. This is your room. Good night."

I stared while Feschian walked away. "Ha!" I called as her shadow merged with the night. "And maybe you're wrong!" To show how little her remark had affected me, I went into my room and slammed the door. Twice.

Strangely, I fell asleep almost immediately. At some point before waking, I dreamt of black-garbed assassins with demon faces who pursued me through a maze that changed from street to castle hall to forest to mountain trail to cavern. No matter where I ran or how quickly, the demon faces followed, steel daggers glittering in their hands.

Something brushed against my shoulder. I snatched a thin wrist and held it tight. My left hand began to drive upward like a spear. "It's me!" gasped Chifeo. I stopped the thrust just short of his neck.

"Sorry," I said, releasing him. "I'm usually not so touchy in the morning."

Chifeo put his hand to his throat and coughed. "I'll, ah, wake you by calling you, next time, Lor— Ah, Rifkin."

"I should've wakened when you entered the room."

"I wish you had, Lor— Rifkin."

"I had a dream. It confused things for me."

"Yes, Rifkin." Chifeo nodded. "I understand." He backed warily out of the room. "A dream."

I made a quick toilet, dunking myself in the shallow bathing pool and shaving with my stiletto. My new clothes proved to be a sleeveless burgundy tunic, a sky-blue cotton shirt with wide sleeves, and indigo pants of wool. I studied the effect in the bathroom's tiled mirror. The colors clashed with my brown belt and boots. Maybe someone would insult my dress. Maybe

Talivane would. Maybe he would decide that I dressed so badly, he should try to kill me. Then I could kill him and convince Naiji to abandon this castle. That cheered me up, until I thought that Talivane might be color-blind. I decided to wear the brown boots anyway, just in case he wasn't.

I left in search of breakfast. A young and freckled red-haired man grinned when I entered the kitchen. I walked in with perfect confidence, so he would know that I belonged here and should be fed. Following a guard's directions, I had already entered the stable, the smithy, and the great hall with the same confidence. "Do you like my boots?" I asked.

"What? Oh. Yes! Very much."

Talivane undoubtedly had more taste.

"So!" said the red-haired man. He wore an apron, which proclaimed him the cook. But then, considering his opinion of my boots, he may only have been eccentric. "Hungry?"

"A little." No one else was present, except for a striped cat and a wolfish dog that slept on the floor near the stone hearth.

"What would you like?" The young man still smiled benignly.

"For breakfast?"

He nodded.

"An ostrich egg," I said, "lightly poached. Two slices of toasted black bread, basted with butter and garlic. Baked potatoes with mushrooms and onions, covered with melted goat's cheese. A large glass of freshly squeezed orange juice, a small glass of cold cow's milk, and a mug of coffee or Dragon's Breath tea."

"Excellent!" said the cook. "I am Dovriex, sometimes called the Tanager. I'm within a year of completing my time as journeyman with the Master Chefs of F'az Borlinash." He bowed.

I smiled, nodding to him. The Master Chefs were famed throughout the Ladizhar Alliance, though it had been close to a century since one had visited the Sea Queen's realm. Perhaps my stay at Castle Gromandiel would have other rewards besides the pleasure of pleasing Naiji.

Dovriex indicated a stool by a wooden table. "Sit. I'll bring your breakfast in an instant, good Rifkin."

I sat. "So. You know of me."

"We're a small group." Dovriex picked up a wooden bowl and went to the stove. "By now everyone knows about Naiji's find." He scooped something from a copper pot into the bowl, then returned and set it before me.

"What's this?" I stared at a tiny quantity of strange grey gruel.

"Your breakfast."

"But I said—"

"I know. For a moment I forgot my own hunger, thinking what joy I'd find in fixing such a meal. And in eating it too. I thank you." He grinned and bowed to me.

"Oh. Right. It was nothing." I tasted a spoonful of the gruel.

"You don't like it?"

"It's amazing," I said, "what a student of the Master Chefs can do with water and grain. Rather old and slightly moldy grain. And no spices at all."

"Actually, I boiled an old sandal, to give it that salty tang."

I hesitated. "A salty tang." I took another bite. "Exactly how I would describe it."

"You like it?"

"It reminds me of the meals my mother prepared, so many years ago."

Dovriex nodded. "As if one of your mother's meals had been buried for all these years, dug up, and presented to you?"

"Uh . . ."

He laughed. "I do my best with what we've got. Maybe you'll like dinner."

"What is it?"

"Bear."

I thought of Avo. Dovriex saw something in my face and nodded sympathetically.

"Avarineo fetched it. I understand—" he began.

"Lady Naiji's still asleep?" I asked.

He accepted the change of subject without difficulty. "Probably. She sleeps late most mornings. She says her magic is tied to the moon."

"Is it?"

"That's just Naiji's way of saying she likes to stay in bed. Magic's only tied to ability."

I nodded. "You people are very free in confiding in me."

He glanced at me, then laughed. "Why not? You'll live or die with us, Rifkin. You might as well know what you can."

"I expected a certain reluctance."

"Because we're witchfolk and you're not? Hardly. If it's any consolation, the witch blood flows so thinly in me that I've yet to manifest any power at all."

"Lady Kivakali called you a seer."

Dovriex shrugged. "Sometimes my dreams seem to mean something. Who can say?"

"Not me," I said. I pushed my bowl away. "Thanks for breakfast."

"If that means you're ready to teach, wait up. I'm joining you."

"Teach?"

Dovriex nodded. "We met last night after you'd gone to bed. Talivane decided on two classes, each attended by half our folk. The rest guard the walls while you instruct us."

"I would've liked to have been consulted."

"Wouldn't we all. That's not Talivane's way."

"You said you met—"

"To discuss. Talivane decides."

"Hmm. Well, if I'm to teach, I'm glad I ate lightly."

"Really? Given the state of the larder, you'll be in ecstasy for days, then."

"Huh. Where's class to be?"

"In the courtyard. Follow me." He folded his apron and left it on a stool. He wore a plain blue tunic and pants of the same hue, and the removal of the apron revealed a belt of reddish leather which matched his ankle-high boots. Lucky him. Four different knives with ivory hilts were held in separate sheaths in a holster on his left hip. The fifth sheath, where the black-hilted knife of the Master Chef would go, was empty. On Dovriex's right was a ceremonial cleaver.

Some said the Master Chefs were a bastard line of the Warrior-Saint's Art. I believed all the schools, whether of killing or calligraphy or meditation or cooking, were the true Art's illegitimate offspring, and none should be thought lower than any other. Still, I wouldn't give Dovriex too much respect until he had prepared a better breakfast for me.

Talivane, a drowsy Naiji, and Chifeo were the only people I recognized in the courtyard. They waited there with eight or nine others, who ranged in age from a girl who had just entered puberty to a white-bearded man who could barely stand erect.

"The elder needn't attend," I said.

"Careful," whispered Dovriex. "That's—"

The old man glared at me. His beard appeared to draw into his face as his toothless lips worked, and then the left side of my body felt as if it had been dipped in lava. I opened my mouth to scream, but managed to gasp, "I'll be delighted to teach him. If he wishes to stay." The pain left as quickly as it had come.

Talivane laughed, and Chifeo tried to hide a snicker. Talivane said, "Rifkin, this is my father, Lord Mondivinaw. He suffered a stroke several years ago, so I rule in his stead. You seem to have discovered that his stroke has, in some ways, heightened his power. When iron is present and he wishes to work magic, he directs a simple spell of sensation to the left side of his victim's body. In the lord's half-paralyzed state, he barely notices the backlash."

I studied the old man carefully. A wooden crutch supported his left arm, and his face, an unhealthy grey, was wrinkled on the right in something like pride or humor. "If I severed the spines of everyone here," I said, "you could rule the world."

Something spoke within my mind: *Very funny, young—*

And, as quickly, something else answered: *Out of my skull, impudent backwoods hedgewizard!*

Naiji was staring at me. Slowly, I realized that the others did so too. "Rifkin?" she said gently, conveying concern, curiosity, and fear.

Talivane had knelt by his father, who lay crumpled on the ground. The old man still breathed, but his breaths were loud and erratic.

"My father..." Talivane gnawed his lip, then began again. "Lord Mondivinaw is the most powerful mindspeaker of us all. Yet you silenced him...."

I wondered who Talivane talked to, until he turned his gaze from his father's face to mine. "What are you, Rifkin? Tell me or I swear that you die in the next instant."

⚛ 10 ⚛

CASTLE
GROMANDIEL

AROUND ME, MOST of the guards had drawn bronze swords and
watched me as if I were some monster. While my wits wrestled
with a thousand frightening possibilities of what had happened
and who the second mindspeaker might be, I said lamely, "I'm
. . . just Rifkin. Rifkin Boundman."

"You're also a witch," said Talivane. The air around his
hands began to sparkle and shimmer as though he wore gloves
made of lightning. "Else you couldn't have felled my father
so easily."

"A witch? Me?" I shook my head. "I don't know what
happened to Lord Mondivinaw, but I had nothing to do with
it."

"He speaks the truth," said Naiji. "I'd know if he didn't. I
looked into his thoughts when I met him."

Talivane glanced at her. "Deeply?"

"Enough to know if he lied."

"I sensed the mindspeech between Rifkin and our father,
only moments ago."

"That's true," I said. "Perhaps the strain was too much for an old man."

"Perhaps." Talivane looked at two red-haired women, twins who might have been Dovriex's sisters. "Take Lord Mondivinaw to his rooms. See that he's comfortable. Let me know if he regains consciousness." He looked back at me. The lightning flared once in his hand. "What did he say to you?"

"He wasn't amused by my comments."

"Is anyone?"

I shrugged.

"What happened then?" Talivane said.

"Our communication ended, and your father fell."

"You stared at him like one who'd lost his wits."

"It's a common reaction to surprise."

"You seemed . . . more than surprised."

"I rarely hear voices in my head, though some might tell you otherwise."

Naiji put her hand on her brother's arm. "You're too suspicious, Talivane. Father's already suffered one stroke. This is probably another. I should go to him."

Talivane nodded slowly. "Go, then."

Naiji glanced at me as she followed the twins who bore her father. Her look told me nothing of her thoughts.

The remaining witches still seemed suspicious, but they also watched nervously around them, hunting for hidden enemies. Chifeo's brow was wrinkled in puzzlement, and Dovriex wore a slight, wary smile.

Talivane said, "Very well." He shook his hand, and the lightning disappeared. "You may begin your class, Rifkin. But remember, you can't hope to deceive witchfolk for long."

"Fine," I said. "Your first lesson, then. So long as the class is in session, address me as Master."

He hesitated. "Or you won't teach?"

"You are quick."

He smiled suddenly. "Then I'll address you as you please, Master Rifkin, for so long as you have anything I wish to learn."

Lucky me. I said, "All right, everyone! Leave your boots and weapons by the wall, then form a line."

No one moved to obey. I stepped over and began unbuckling my sword belt. Dovriex, saying nothing, joined me. Then

Talivane and Chifeo followed, and then the others. Naiji and the twins returned while my students were still ridding themselves of shoes and weapons.

"Da sleeps," she told Talivane. "I think he'll recover."

"Thank the gods," said Talivane. "We need him."

The class formed a ragged line before me on a cold, bare patch of ground in the courtyard. I was glad for a bright morning sun. I studied each of my students. Chifeo and Dovriex appeared eager, but I could not read Talivane's face. Naiji seemed proud of me, or possibly amused. The two red-haired women were impatient, perhaps a little dubious of learning anything useful from a dark little foreigner. The rest, two boys and a pretty girl about Chifeo's age, a burly man, a middle-aged woman as stout as the man, and a thin, balding fellow of Talivane's age, were still mistrustful of me. Obviously they were only here because Talivane had ordered it.

I smiled as though I had perfect control of my class. "You may already know my name. It is Rifkin Teacher. You'll address me as Master in any matter concerning the Art, and at all times when we gather to learn it together. I do not claim the title for any ability of mine, or because I demand your respect. When we gather, I represent the Warrior-Saint's teaching. All courtesy done to me is done to her, as is all discourtesy. Lack of respect will not be punished. It will merely be acknowledged, and the discourteous one will be dismissed from this class. Is that understood?"

They all nodded.

I said, "Say, 'Yes, Master.'"

"Yes, Master," they answered in unison, even Talivane.

I smiled. I liked teaching. "Good. Then this is the first lesson for you all. In the short time we have, you cannot hope to learn any tricks that'll aid you in battling the Duke's warriors."

"What? This is a waste of time?" said Talivane.

I scratched my neck, looked at my fingernail, then looked at him. "Did I say that?"

"No."

I waited.

"Master."

I smiled again. I considered telling him that true study of the Art did not end when a class was dismissed. "You'll learn no tricks. But if you listen, and study, and learn, you may be able to act more efficiently in times of stress." I thought about my own behavior since I had arrived at Castle Gromandiel and said, "Then again, you may not."

Talivane raised an eyebrow in question, though he nodded.

"Master?" asked Naiji. Her smile at the name was such that I had difficulty restraining mine.

"Yes?"

"What is this Art?"

"It's a way of life. Some say it's the best way for people to live, but the truth is that it's only one of many paths to a goal, and not a goal in itself."

"And what's the goal?"

I shrugged. "I rarely know where I'm going. I just choose the road that looks easiest."

A few students chuckled. Naiji said, "That's no answer."

"True. If you're lucky, you'll find one for yourself." I looked around. "Have any of you studied fencing?"

The older man nodded. His moustache was thin, flecked with white, and the hair at his temples had receded. A scar was etched along his left cheek, which was the reason I had asked about fencing.

I said, "Why did you choose to study the sword?"

He smiled coldly. "Because a witch cannot defend himself with a harp."

I might have told him that would depend on the harpist, but he would not understand. I said, "And has anyone studied dance?"

Chifeo raised his hand.

"Ah. Why?"

"It's pretty."

Several of the others laughed. "A good reason," I told him.

The pretty girl of Chifeo's age said, "I also dance, Master." Her smile suggested she was thinking of a more private ballet.

"Why?"

"Because I enjoy learning the things my body can do."

Dovriex said, "I'd enjoy learning the things your body can do."

The girl laughed with the others. "Dovriex," I said quickly, trying to maintain some semblance of classroom spirit. "You wish to become a Master Chef. Why?"

"Because I like to eat."

The stout woman laughed. "That's why *I'd* become a chef, but you're too thin, Tanager."

Dovriex cocked his head to one side, then said, "But I do like to eat. And cooking's an easy life."

The woman said, "You may think so. I'll stay a rocksmith."

Talivane said, "Good. I've eaten your bread. I thought I'd eaten one of your stones."

When the others chuckled, Naiji said, "I'm glad Dovriex cooks for us."

Dovriex said, "Thank you! Oh. You slept through breakfast."

I began to consider abandoning the oblique approach. One more try, I told myself. "You!" I said to the stout man. "What do you do to earn your keep?"

"I transform myself into a panther and chase away annoyances."

I imagined he would make a rather plump panther. I only said, "Oh."

"I'm good at it."

"I'm sure. That's why you do it?"

He looked suspicious, but nodded. "In part."

"And?"

"It's a living."

"And?"

He grimaced. "Are you going to teach us to fight or are you going to keep asking questions?"

"What do you expect?"

"I don't know."

Chifeo said, "I do!" We all looked at him. He blushed. "Well, I thought there'd be, you know . . ."

"No," I said.

"Well, sitting around with our legs crossed and thinking about nothingness, and riddles, and—"

"Ah," I said. "Like, what's the sound of one hand clapping?" I snapped my fingers as an answer. "Or is it masturbation? Or is the only answer the sound of slapping whoever asks the question?"

Naiji said, "You're saying that there are many answers to every question."

"In part."

"There's more?"

I nodded.

"So tell us."

I laughed. "What would anything mean, that I told you?"

"It would mean that you thought . . ." Her eyes narrowed as she grew suspicious.

I nodded again.

"You want us to find the answer ourselves, so we'll believe it."

"Yes."

"But there are so many answers."

"Yes."

Chifeo shouted. "There are different answers for each of us!"

I sighed my relief. "Exactly."

The shape-shifter said, "I didn't come here to think."

"If you don't like it," said Dovriex, "pity Avarineo in the next class."

Talivane said, "This lesson seems rather simplistic."

"Odd, then, that you weren't first with any answers." I looked at the others and wondered what I hoped to accomplish. I doubted I could teach enough of the Art to give us even a tiny advantage in the upcoming conflict. Perhaps I only wanted to earn the witches' respect and trust. Finding no answer that satisfied me, I decided to simply teach them as though they were any other group who met to learn the Art.

I led them through several exercises. Their life in these hills had made them strong, so I concentrated on stretching and relaxing their muscles. The casual chatter ended as the physical work began. I demonstrated the basic kicks and punches and blocks, and let them practice a few fighting techniques with each other.

The dancers, Chifeo and the pretty girl, showed promise, if they decided to continue their studies. So did Naiji and Dovriex. I wondered what went into training a Master Chef. The rocksmith had a sense of perseverance that would help her in the early stages of learning, but the red-haired twins were almost ideal students, being limber and strong, quick to see an action, understand it, and make it their own.

Talivane, on the other hand, was too tense. I told him twice to relax his shoulders, then decided that twice was once too often for a first class. The fencer tried too hard and therefore did poorly. His pride demanded that he be perfect with a single attempt. The other man, the self-proclaimed shape-shifter, moved with grace but without power. His punches and blocks were pleasant to see, yet meant nothing.

Sometime in the second hour of practice, Chifeo said, "Master?"

"Yes."

"Would you show us what we're to learn?"

"I've been doing exactly that."

"I don't mean like that. I mean, would you give us an exhibition of how an Artist fights?"

"The Art may teach fighting, but fighting isn't its goal."

Chifeo ignored that. "Please?"

The others smiled and nodded. In part, I knew from experience, they only wanted to rest, and watching the teacher would give them an excuse to sit. The rocksmith was flushed with exertion, and Talivane's breathing was loud. I remembered how I had enjoyed seeing those who knew more of the Art than I did, and how grateful I had been for the opportunity to sit. "Very well," I said. "I'll need a volunteer."

They glanced at each other. Chifeo, after a moment, hesitantly raised his hand.

"Fine," I said. "It was your idea."

"What do I do?" He seemed to regret his impulse. He looked at the ground and wiped his hands nervously on his pants.

"Fight me. And don't worry. I'll stop each technique just before I hit you."

Chifeo nodded. "I don't think I can control—"

"That's all right. I can defend myself." A few of the others laughed, thinking I had spoken modestly. But then, I thought I had spoken modestly too.

"Good," said Chifeo. A hint of a smile came to his lips, more than would normally come from a nervous student facing his teacher before a group of his peers. I should have seen that as a warning. I only thought he felt cocky facing someone of approximately his own size.

Chifeo circled me, holding his arms in an awkward parody of mine. I followed him with my eyes and only turned when he was about to pass beyond my sight. He finally came at me with a double-strike at my face and midriff, a punching technique that I had shown the class. I blocked and countered with a hand thrust that would have driven his nose into his brain, He gasped as he dodged back. The audience gasped also. I congratulated myself. Old Rifkin's the greatest against untrained children.

Chifeo tried a side-kick at my face. He was limber, which I credited to his dance training, but the kick was clumsy and slow. I leaned away from it, then darted in for a hammerhand blow to his skull. He ducked, flailing his arms and kicking again so wildly that he should have fallen. Instead, his foot struck my ribs. Only an instinctive block saved me from a crushed chest, but I still coughed in pain and surprise.

Chifeo's eyes went wide. "Are you hurt, Master?"

"Only my pride," I said. "Continue." I am a very slow learner.

My right side ached more than I wanted to acknowledge. I shifted so that my left was to him, then stepped in close to sweep his feet from under him. I had decided to end this practice bout quickly.

His forward foot lifted a bit, seemingly by coincidence, and came down on my ankle. I twisted to keep from breaking it. That meant falling, so I turned, and wrenching my leg free, somersaulted out of Chifeo's way.

He laughed, apparently in innocent enjoyment at doing well in a friendly fight, as he skipped forward to kick at my head. His heel grazed my skull, dazing me. I reacted at last as I was trained, as though this were an actual battle and not a teaching demonstration that, for some reason, had gone wrong. My hand came up to snatch Chifeo's ankle. It closed on air. He was faster than I was.

It made no sense to me. I am a *very* slow learner. Chifeo came in with another punch, a blow that must have seemed harmless to the observers. It barely touched me, but it glanced against a nerve in my left arm, paralyzing it. I understood then. The boy's performance, no matter what it looked like, was due to more than his good fortune or my bad. Chifeo was not what he seemed. Which meant—

I warded off a kick that almost ended any of my future hopes of fatherhood. Chifeo laughed, again innocently, and said, "This is fun, Master!" The class laughed, too, a little nervously. Several of them had begun to wonder if I was clowning or, worse, if I was not as skilled as I had seemed. I was alone in knowing just how much fun Chifeo was having.

I didn't know if he wanted to kill me because he had recognized me or if he thought I would be in his way when it was time to shuck his role of servant and slay the Gromandiels. It didn't matter. He had chosen an interesting ploy, to make me appear less competent than I was, then to kill me with an "accidental" blow that a "real master" would have deflected. He had overplayed his hand by trying too hard to prove my inability. I shouted, "Chifeo's a Spir—"

And then, for that crucial instant, my mouth seemed to fill with cotton. I opened my lips, but I could not speak, or even grunt. I thought Chifeo's smile grew slightly wider to show his satisfaction with his skill and his subtlety, though that may have been my imagination. I realized with the horror that slows time that Chifeo had infiltrated the witchfolk on his own merits as a witch. During that long moment, I watched as he skipped forward, ready to silence me forever.

And then he fainted.

Naiji stared at Chifeo, unconscious on the ground. "Oh, Rifkin. Not again."

"Two," said Talivane with a sigh. "I don't know why, Rifkin, but you aren't at all subtle. Do you really think to dupe us twice in as many hours?"

I faced a ring of grim, unsympathetic faces. "Wait!" I cried. "Did anyone sense any mindspeaking? Any at all?"

No one answered, though they all continued to stare.

"Or any use of witchcraft coming from me? Any? I know you're all suspicious enough to have watched me closely."

Talivane grunted grudgingly, "No."

"Good," I said. "Chifeo tried a gagging spell on me. It didn't work."

Talivane's eyes narrowed. "Why—"

"Why didn't it work?" I asked, to stave off the question Talivane had begun to answer. "Not because I'm some master magician, as you seem to suspect. I have iron hidden on me." Not for the first time, I was glad I'd kept the pin in my hair. "His spell must have rebounded from it."

Talivane said, "But why would Chifeo use magic in a demonstration bout? It doesn't make any sense."

"Because he's a spy and probably a Spirit." As one member of my audience gasped at my words, I said, "You may have thought you had your share of problems, Gromandiel, but it looks to me like they've only just begun."

≫ 11 ≪

CASTLE
GROMANDIEL

"THIS CLASS IS over." I bowed to my students to dismiss them. They hesitated, but Naiji nodded and said, "Go."

The fencer said, "If the foreigner's—"

"We're safe with Rifkin."

I wondered at her certainty. The fencer said, "Lady, if you're wrong—"

"You think I could be?"

Her question was phrased innocently enough, but the man stiffened as though slapped. Dovriex said, "Lady, he's only concerned for you."

"And I appreciate his concern. Still, leave us."

With many backward glances, the others went. When Talivane and Naiji and I were alone, he said, "Tell me about it."

"Chifeo's a spy."

"So say you."

"He's a Spirit."

"Again, so—"

"He fights too well for a serving boy."

"That?" Talivane gestured at the ground where we'd fought. "He was lucky, but—"

"Too lucky."

Talivane's eyes narrowed. "I do tire of your interruptions."

"Well, la-de-da."

Naiji put her hand on my arm. It seemed to be a favorite gesture of hers. Since it often led to such nice things, I let her hand lie there. "Rifkin, you're just—"

"Upset? Me? Rifkin Merryman?"

"Rifkin, you think you embarrassed yourself—"

"I think I almost died."

"But—"

"Wait." I looked at them both. "Am I not at least minimally competent in matters of physical defense?"

Talivane stroked his chin. "I had thought so, until I saw you fighting the boy."

"Mother and Son, are you blind as well as stupid?"

Talivane glared. "I—"

"Oops." I raised my hands peacefully. "Sorry."

Naiji said, "Rifkin Tactlord rides again."

"Look," I said. "I'll tell you a simple truth. Chifeo shouldn't have been able to touch me, let alone hurt me."

"We saw," said Talivane with thick sarcasm.

"You saw his show," I said. "And you believed it. But if you doubt my ability, I'll duel with you here, bare hands against bare hands. Tell me then whether I know anything of the Art."

"We saw you against the Spirits last night," Naiji said.

"I didn't say I know a lot about the Art."

She moved her hand from my wrist to my shoulder. "You fought well, then."

Talivane frowned. Either the question of Chifeo's loyalty disturbed him, or he didn't like being reminded that his sister had found a playmate. He said, "Perhaps the boy was lucky."

"Too lucky. I tell you again, he used magic against me."

"I sensed something that might have been a spell," Talivane admitted.

"Good. Now, why would he do that?"

"If he did it."

"If he did it," I granted.

"He was scared?" Naiji suggested.

"Did he look scared to you? He's a Spirit."

"I thought Spirits don't use magic."

"This one does."

"That doesn't make sense."

"I'm not trying to make sense. I'm trying to tell the truth."

"Enough of this," said Talivane. "Naiji will learn what's true when he recovers."

She nodded. I noted that if truth-telling was so easy for her, I had another reason to suspect their story of questioning a prisoner during the middle of the night. Then I realized that even if Naiji could recognize truth, she might not be able to make someone speak it. Unless, as she had hinted, she could actually hunt among memories. I did not want to consider that last possibility.

Talivane said, "You know a lot about Spirits."

I shrugged. "I've dealt with them before."

"But the boy surprised you."

"Yes."

"Why? If you're so competent—"

"I've never known them to employ spies. Nor have I known them to use magic."

Talivane laughed. "And yet you suspect Chifeo? This is a very feeble tale, Rifkin. I continue to suspect you, for all that my sister may trust you."

"I've heard rumors that the Spirits keep a few witch-slaves in steel bonds and force them to obey."

"Chifeo's hardly kept in bonds."

"Even so, he's a Spirit. I'd know."

Talivane frowned and studied me. "They've pursued you?"

"Yes."

"Why?"

"For something that happened in the south. Several years ago."

"And you've lived this long?"

I put my right hand against my left wrist to check my pulse. "Yes."

Talivane sighed. "I've known many who were reluctant to speak of their past, but you must be the most reluctant of all."

"We all excel at something."

"Why didn't you tell us about this?"

"I believed they no longer hunted me." Or at least I had hoped it, and hoped it still.

Talivane nodded. "And, last night, when I showed you my visitors?"

"They were after you and Lady Naiji. So you said, and so they acted."

"A fine distinction."

"All distinctions are fine ones."

"Careful," Naiji warned Talivane. "Don't get him started on philosophy."

"No," Talivane agreed. "Let's look in on Chifeo."

"So soon?" I asked.

"If your explanation is correct, and I'm not saying it is, it would mean he only used a very small spell. The effects of the presence of iron would have faded by now."

We donned our shoes and swords, then walked into the castle. I said, "What happens if Naiji learns nothing from him?"

"She'll learn something."

The infirmary was a large room, and very warm from a fire that burned in a central hearth. One of the red-haired twins was telling Chifeo to lie still while she held a damp cloth against his forehead. Mondivinaw occupied a second pallet. He still slept. Each of his breaths was followed by a pause so long that each subsequent breath surprised me.

Chifeo glanced at us, then turned his head away and began to cry softly.

Talivane looked at Mondivinaw. "The lord . . ."

The red-haired woman said, "No change."

"Did you strip Chifeo?" I asked.

"Yes," said his nurse.

"Find anything unusual?"

"His socks are clean."

"That's not what I meant by unusual."

"If you knew Chifeo, it would be."

"Maybe. I doubt that any of you knew him."

"He's been with us for almost a year," said Naiji.

"So?" I addressed the boy. "There's no point in pretending any longer, Chifeo." I switched to the trade tongue of the Ladizhar, a language known to all Spirits. "Your role is discovered. Your commission cannot be fulfilled. There is no shame, only—"

He spun on the pallet, flipping a long splinter of the bed's frame at my throat. I deflected it with the edge of my hand.

"I'm ready for you, youth," I said. "Your guile is greater than that of the Spirits who followed you, but you are no more successful."

"What are you?" he gasped in the same language.

"Rifkin," I said. "Rifkin Outcast."

He shook his head. "You're Izla."

His certainty surprised me, but I only said "No." I remembered how quietly he had come to wake me this morning and realized that the duel in the courtyard was not his first attempt to murder me.

"Talivane will kill me," he said.

"Perhaps."

"You're Izla. I was right to act." His face grew desperate. "Tell me that much. Please."

I hesitated, then said, "In Istviar, I would be recognized as the Seaprince."

"I knew it!" After a moment, he said, "You're more skilled than the Masters think."

"Obviously. I'm still alive."

"You deserve to die."

"Why? You think I'm what you are?"

"Yes."

"It's no shame, Chifeo. You've lived with your own kind for months, now. Aren't they people, like any other?"

"So they pretend."

Someone else might convince him. I knew I would not.

"What's he saying?" asked Naiji.

I wanted to walk to the window and stare at the clouds, but I could not turn away for fear that Chifeo would attack one of us. "He's a Spirit," I said.

"The trick with that bit of wood told us as much," said Talivane. "Yet he has some skill at transmutation."

"He's also a witch," I said.

They waited for me to explain. The red-haired woman appeared to have deduced enough to know what we discussed. Chifeo only cried softly. His gasps were interrupted by Mondivinaw's ragged inhalations. At last I said, "I suspect the Spirits raised him. I've heard they sometimes do that with the children of their victims, though I've never heard of it happening with witch babies. His mother was probably slain when he was born, and he was taught what they believe."

"He told you all that?" asked Naiji.

"More or less."

"What was he doing here, then?"

"If the Spirits wanted a Master Witch to serve them, who better than a witch to train a witch? And here he could be their spy as well. How do you think last night's visitors found Talivane so easily?"

The Count's hands began to flicker with lightning. "One last question, Rifkin. If this is true, why wasn't Chifeo our executioner? Why did they bother to send the others?"

That only took a moment of thought. I said, "Because the boy's teaching is incomplete. The others came to kill you two, and only you two. That'd end whatever threat this stronghold offers to Komaki. Chifeo could continue his studies with the remaining witches, even if they fled this castle. Am I right, Chifeo?"

He continued to cry quietly.

Naiji studied the boy. "He must hate very much."

"He does."

Chifeo snapped up from the bed and pointed to me. "Do you know what he is? He's Izla Seaprince!" He uttered the name in Ladizhan.

"What?" said Talivane.

"It's a traditional southern expression," I said. "It means I'm a wonderfully clever fellow."

"He's a witch!" cried Chifeo. "The most powerful witch who ever lived!"

"It's too late for flattery," I said.

"Hmm? What of the iron that Rifkin wears?" Talivane asked.

"A disguise! Can't you see! The perfect disguise! He's worse than all of you combined!"

I waggled my fingers by my ear to suggest that Chifeo's brains had leaked from his skull. Talivane ignored me. He said, "An interesting claim."

I said, "One that's easily disproved."

"How!" demanded Chifeo.

I turned to Talivane. "Tell me the words to a very simple spell. I'll recite it while wearing my weapons. You'll see whether there's any backlash."

Talivane said, "Very well." He told me to repeat several syllables, which I did.

"See?" I said. "No backlash."

"You should be glad," Naiji said. "That was an impotence spell."

Chifeo stared at me. "But you said—"

"It's a long story," I answered in the coastal tongue. "I'm as human as you wish you were."

"But—"

"Maybe I'll write a book about it someday."

Talivane's hands glowed brightly with lightning. I wondered if he would try to kill the boy then, and whether I would try to stop him. The Count said, "To the dungeons, Chifeo. You know the way." He glanced at the red-headed nurse. "Accompany us. With your sword ready."

"Of course," the woman said.

They took Chifeo away. Wondering if I had done well or badly, I turned to Naiji and said, "What now?"

She kissed me lightly on the lips. "I've things to do. Amuse yourself."

"Amuse myself. Right. I'd tell myself stories, but I've heard every one I know."

"You're inventive. You'll think of something."

I did. I returned to my quarters, and for a long moment, watched my hands shake. I had told Talivane I did not like Death; I hated her most when she offered to couple with me. Then, aware that I stank of fear and hard work, I bathed. I wished Naiji would join me. Forgetting myself in the art of love would have been nice. Holding someone and saying nothing would have been nicer still.

The lives of too many strangers had been linked to mine. I found myself hoping that Mondivinaw would remain in his coma until I had learned the identity of the second mindspeaker. Mondivinaw would certainly think the voice had been mine. And Chifeo inhabited the dungeons, thanks to my intervention. Talivane, I was sure, did not keep him there to free him later. When Chifeo was slain, I would share the responsibility.

I dressed again. My belt and boots looked no better with the blue and burgundy clothing than they had before, but perhaps concerns of dress were not noticed when survival was the primary issue. I wandered through the deserted halls in search of the dungeons. The castle was slightly smaller than it had seemed the night before, yet it was large enough. The doors to several wings had been sealed, seemingly for centuries. Studying one near Talivane's quarters, I met Captain Feschian.

"Lost?" Feschian asked.

"No. I forgot to ask what you think of my boots."

"You shouldn't wear them with those pants."

I considered that for a moment. "I agree."

"What're you doing here?"

"Trying to make sure no one sees me in these boots."

"You've been wearing them all day."

"Oh. Well, I was exploring, so I won't get lost again."

"You shouldn't have told me that."

"Why not?"

"You won't have an excuse when next I find you where you shouldn't be."

"And where shouldn't I be?"

"Give it up, Rifkin."

"But if I don't know—"

"Don't come by Talivane's rooms at night."

I nodded. "Talivane's rooms. At night. Don't come. Got it."

"You're sure? If you'd like, I'll repeat it more slowly."

"Repeat what?"

"Very funny."

"Tell me, how do I find the dungeons?"

"Come by Talivane's rooms at night."

"Very funny," I said, mimicking her voice.

She smiled. "Why do you want to know?"

"I'd like to question the Spirits you captured."

"They won't speak to us."

"I think I can convince them."

"You'll tell me if you get any answers?"

"Of course."

She considered this, then nodded. "Go left at the corridor that passes the grand hall. You'll find a heavy door of teak on your right. Behind that lie the stairs to the dungeons. Tell the guard I said you could talk with the prisoners."

"Thanks." I left her and continued on. Enough time had passed by then that I decided to seek the dining room instead of the dungeons. I found my way easily after asking directions at the stable, the seamster's rooms, and the armorer's. Soon I took a seat near an end of the long oak table and discovered that I had earned so much respect from this morning's endeavors that no one would sit uninvited near me.

The young girl from my first class brought a bowl of stew and a mug of weak tea.

"Thanks," I said. "Want to sit with me?"

Without answering, she hurried on. I cursed myself for phrasing the question too subtly.

I tasted the stew. Dovriex might become a Master Chef someday. He had found a few tubers that resembled carrots and thickened the broth with ground grain. Then I recognized the flavor of bear. It was not easy for me to eat something I had known by name, even though I hadn't learned its name until after its death. By evening my hunger might be sufficient to stifle my qualms. For now I wasn't hungry.

I thought I would sit there and show that I did not feel excluded from the witches' company. An old hound wandered out from the kitchen and passed by me. I gave him a chunk of the meat from my stew. He ate it and stayed near. Dogs are noble, discerning animals. I gave the selfless beast another morsel. He continued to sit near me.

Naiji, Talivane, Feschian, and a few others were speaking together at the far end of the table. Kivakali sat by Talivane, staring downward into her lap. The others ignored her. Perhaps there were worse things than sitting alone.

When Naiji glanced at me, I waggled my fingers at her. She continued talking to the others. I went outside. The hound chose to follow me. At the door I slipped it a few more pieces of bear meat. It continued to follow me. A truly fine dog.

Captain Feschian and the giant, Avarineo, were in my afternoon class. The rest were guards and seemingly ordinary folk, probably farmers or weavers before they came to join Talivane's crusade to restore the Witches' Empire.

Feschian said, "When will you begin?"

I looked over my students and saw who was missing. "When Lady Kivakali joins us."

"She won't."

"Then I won't begin." I folded my arms.

"It's Talivane's wish that you teach."

"It's my wish to teach everyone. Everyone includes your master's wife."

"Perhaps the lady does not wish to study war."

"Perhaps a ship's cat does not wish to swim, yet that's an art it should learn if it's to go to sea."

Feschian nodded. "I'll speak with Lady Kivakali."

"Thank you."

We waited in silence for the captain's return. I wondered if any of my students had yet to hear about Mondivinaw and Chifeo. The day had grown warmer, so I loosened my jacket. Naiji claimed the cold would return, but this weather felt like spring to me.

Kivakali walked beside Feschian. Her hair was bound in two braids, and she came barefoot, wearing only a sleeveless tunic and loose pants, both the color of sand. Her hair was tied back with a green ribbon.

"You've studied the Art?" I asked, indicating her headband.

She nodded, blushing. "My father hired a teacher, when I was younger."

"Then you should have been prompt."

"I didn't, um, know I'd have time." Which meant Talivane did not wish it, of course. Kivakali smiled almost flirtatiously at me and looked quickly away. I realized that our roles in Castle Gromandiel were very similar, both of us outsiders, neither of us witches, both of us bound by vows rather than love. I had my skills and my steel weapons to make the witch-folk treat me reasonably well. Kivakali had nothing.

The class went smoothly enough, excepting Avarineo's occasional comment. His first was, "If we're here to study art, where's paper and charcoal?" That amused the giant sufficiently that he asked it twice. His second was, "Why should we learn to fight? When enemy comes, we'll just say teacher's name. They'll run away with their noses covered, afraid of smelling farts."

Shortly after that I asked him to serve me as my model. "Sure," he said. "Teacher will draw me?" He guffawed.

Remembering the surprises Chifeo had given me, I told him to stand perfectly still while I demonstrated a few techniques. I kicked near his head a couple of times to warm up, and his long hair whipped nicely with the popping of air. He flinched when my heel stopped at the tip of his nose and stayed there long enough for him to focus on it. I punched and kicked at thirty vulnerable parts of his body in fifteen seconds or so, then quit. Avarineo stood like a wide-eyed statue for the entire exhibition. Afterward he said, "You may have a funny name, R-r-rifkin, but I will treat you as my friend now, for certain." Then his eyes grew huge as he thought about what he had said. He added, "I planned to treat you as a friend all the time, just like Lady Naiji said. Of course. But now I plan to treat you *even more* as my friend. Much more as my friend. A whole lot—" I told him that I understood and appreciated this, which appeared to please him.

There were several in this class who might someday be Artists. The most promising was a girl of seven or eight, who did everything with an expression of perfect seriousness. Captain Feschian had obviously studied with some school before. Her technique was competent but uninspired, as if she had learned what she knew long ago and had practiced alone since then.

Kivakali seemed too self-conscious to show what she might really be able to do. She often confused the order of the moves when I told the class to practice specific combinations. I suspected that she had only stayed with her earlier teacher for a few months. At one point she apologized for being so awkward. All I could tell her was to concentrate less on how others saw her and more on what she was doing.

When the afternoon class ended, I went again in search of the dungeons. The first likely door that I tried was to a bath occupied by an older woman from the class I had just dismissed. Her subsequent instructions were useless for finding the dungeons but did much to increase my knowledge of the witches' dialect.

The dungeons, when I found them, were damp and cold. The Gromandiels had done little to maintain them. The teak door's leather hinges protested being opened. The stairs themselves were worn and moss-encrusted, ready to pitch a careless climber to a fatal fall. My torch, taken from the hall, barely burned in the stale, fetid air. Its light seemed to shine no more than a foot or two before me as I descended.

"Who goes there?" demanded a nervous guard. He jumped up from the low bench on which he had rested, or perhaps slept.

"Rifkin," I said. "Rifkin Inquisitor."

"What do you want?"

"Love, security, and the respect of those who know me."

"I mean, what do you want here?"

"Oh. You should have said that."

"I did!"

"So you did. I want to speak with your prisoners. Feschian said I might."

"One of them's in a coma and can't be roused."

"It must be contagious."

"What?"

"Never mind."

"He put himself into a death-trance," the guard whispered confidingly. "They can do that, you know."

"I'd heard."

"You want to see the serving boy too?"

"No. Just the others."

He nodded, then unlocked a door behind him. "Remember, I'll be listening to everything you say."

"I'm always best with an audience."

The room beyond was larger than the guard's chamber. It was also darker, danker, and a thousand times worse in odor. Three Spirits, all wearing their black assassin's garb, were manacled to the walls. Their chains appeared to be shiny brass, the only new things in this part of Castle Gromandiel. One spirit lay slack on the mucky floor. The other two, fastened to different walls, turned their faces away from the torch in my hand.

"Greetings," I said in Ladizhan. "Anyone feel like betraying the masters on Goon Isle?"

"Moon Isle!" said one, a young girl.

"You, eh? Excellent. To begin, who hired you?"

She turned away and said nothing.

I sighed. "That was short." I turned to the other, a boy of Chifeo's age with a wispy beard. "How about you? Will you talk?"

"No."

"Hah! You just did." When that clever ploy failed, I said, "I can offer you something."

"What?"

"A quick death now. That's more than the witches promise."

"I'm not afraid of pain."

"I heard your companion die last night. I hope he wasn't afraid of pain either."

"He wasn't."

"Good for him. The Gromandiels tortured him for hours. He wasn't afraid of mutilation either?"

The Spirit closed his eyes.

"The Gromandiels are witches," I said. "Of course, you knew that."

"Of course."

"And you've thought about what witches can do to make you talk, I suppose. Change you into something vile and strange..." I walked away and examined some of the scratchings on the wall. "Look here!" I improvised. "Oh, You can't. Sorry. It seems someone started a poem. 'There once was a witch from the east, who was fond both of man and of beast—' That's all. Maybe you'll have time to finish it before the Gromandiels start on you. But I doubt it."

I walked to the door, then turned back. "You may think I'm not being very understanding, but I am. See my sword?" I drew it halfway to show them the steel. "I'm as human as you are. I wouldn't want those witches to toy with me. You'd think they'd let you die human, but I doubt they'll even let you have that little bit of dignity. Back at Moon Isle, your fellows will probably say..." I walked up to the male. "What's your name?"

He spat at me.

I jumped back. "Spittle, then. They'll probably say, remember young Spittle? Died as a slug. Horrible thing, dying as a slug. Me, I'd take an honorable death any day. But not young Spittle. Maybe he wanted to be a slu—"

"Shut up!"

"Maybe Spittle wasn't a real human at all. Maybe his mother had a thing for witches."

The boy lunged at me as if he expected to tear his chains from the wall.

"It's your choice," I said. "Tell me who sent you, and die human. Or die as a mangled thing, knowing that word will travel through every holding of Spirit Dancers of your incompetence."

"Why?"

I gave him a cruel grin. "Because I'll tell everyone I meet of the young Spirit with the mole on his left cheek. I'll tell how he gave away his entire band with his clumsiness, then begged pathetically to be spared."

"It'll be a lie!"

"True. So?"

"I can't trust you."

"I don't blame you. But you know what the witches offer. Mutilation, transformation ... They'll learn more from you than I need to know, Spirit. They'll learn all that I'd ask of you, and then they'll learn everything that ever shamed you. Then they'll laugh at you, toy with you—"

"What of her?" He indicated the girl, who listened with a sneer.

"She'll tell no tales."

"You'll be quick?"

"Yes."

"With her too?"

"Yes."

The girl cried to him, "Don't—"

"Lady Kivakali hired us."

I nodded as though this did not surprise me, then turned to go.

"Wait! Our bargain!"

I shook my head.

His eyes widened. "But—"

"Lord Death may be your best friend, but I won't send you to him."

"You lied!"

"Yes."

"You vile, dung-eating—" His face was contorted in rage and frustration.

"Call me an honorless bit of slime," I suggested. "That's what I feel like."

I left him cursing in the dark.

12

CASTLE GROMANDIEL

THE GUARD GLARED at me as I closed the cell door. "You spoke in a foreign tongue!"

"Did I?" I shook my head in sympathy. "Mother and Son, southerners are sneaky."

"What'd you tell them?"

"That'd I'd kill them if they would tell me who hired them." He laughed. "I can't imagine that was effective."

"No." I started up the stairs. "Probably not."

Captain Feschian waited for me in the hall. I nodded at her and moved to pass by, but she shifted to block me.

"What'd they tell you?"

"You listened?"

"Yes."

"How?"

"Never mind that. What'd they say?"

"I didn't think you just happened to be visiting the cells while I was."

"No, Rifkin. What did they say?"

"Exactly?"

"Yes."

"Very well." I began to repeat the Spirit's story in Ladizhan.

She sighed. "Don't play with me, Rifkin. Talivane may be the only one of us who can use his power directly against someone wearing iron—"

"What about Mondivinaw?"

"You're a stickler for details."

I shrugged. "I try to keep things straight."

"An unending battle, I'm sure." Before I could say anything, she continued. "Understand this, Rifkin. There are ways for a witch to kill someone near iron. For example, I could loosen the stones over your head. The backlash would make me nauseous, but you'd still be dead."

"I'll keep that in mind."

"I don't enjoy threatening you, Rifkin. But even Talivane will seem more patient than I am if you frustrate me in my duty."

"Which is?"

"To protect the people in this castle."

"What am I, a tree?"

"Rifkin." Something in her voice reminded me of Naiji speaking to Avarineo.

"You're right. I'm sorry."

"I don't know what you are, but I'd like to think you're a part of us. Do me a favor and help me believe it."

"And what's Kivakali? Is she a part of 'us'?"

"She's Talivane's wife."

I shook my head. "That's not an answer."

Her eyes narrowed. "The Spirits implicated her?"

"The boy did. He said she hired them."

"That's all he said?"

"I thought it was enough."

"I wish Naiji'd been there to listen for truth."

"I doubt I could get him to repeat it."

Feschian fingered an old scar that ran along her jaw. "Did you believe him?"

I thought about that for a long moment. "I don't know. I'd rather not."

She nodded. "So would I."

"Could Kivakali have had the chance to hire Spirits?"

"I don't know."

"You could guess," I said.

"Hmm." Feschian looked at me, then said reluctantly, "She might have."

"And the inclination?"

Feschian looked away.

I said, "You've seen how Talivane treats her."

"Yes."

"Well, then?"

"I almost wouldn't blame her, if she tried," Feschian said. Then her features grew harsher. "I'd still stop her."

"Of course."

Feschian said, "The Spirits' leader said Talivane and Naiji were their targets. That doesn't mean they were their only targets."

I glanced at her.

She said, "Who'll you tell?"

"Naiji."

She understood. "Your bond."

"Yes."

Cautiously, Feschian said, "We shouldn't do the Spirits' work for them."

I stared, and she nodded slowly. Her message was plain enough. If the Gromandiels thought Kivakali might be their enemy, Kivakali would die. But if I told no one and Kivakali was truly an enemy, Naiji might die.

"What do you want me to do?" I said.

"Trust me. Tell no one. Watch Kivakali. And guard Naiji. That's all."

"May I sleep and eat as well?"

"In your spare time."

"Spare time. Right."

"Well?"

"I'll watch Kivakali."

"What'll you tell Naiji?"

"To trust no one."

Feschian studied me, then smiled. "You're a good man, Rifkin."

"Everyone says so." I stepped by her.

"Dinner'll be ready soon."

"We eat later in the south."

"I doubt anyone'll save your share."

"Dinner sounds like a good idea, now that you mention it."

Actually I was far from hungry, for the taste of the business in the dungeons was still thick in my mouth. I only said that to see if Feschian would smile, and she did. The lines around her eyes deepened. She had never been a beauty, and her broken nose should have made her ugly, but her strength and her character made her face very pleasant to look upon.

I started to walk toward the dining hall. Feschian stopped me with a hand on my shoulder and jerked her head in the other direction. "This way."

"I'll never learn my way around here."

"We're not going to dinner yet. Come."

"Where?"

"Come."

I shrugged and followed. We went outside, into the empty courtyard, and climbed the broad, stone stairs to the rear wall where Castle Gromandiel butted against the cliff. I looked up, seeing only bare rock, and higher up, the snow line. I turned and looked west. The sun was close to setting. A few clouds made swatches of pink and purple across the sky. The valley was already dark, though several naked tree tops caught the sun's last rays to shine like silver sculptures in the sea of evergreens.

"It's pretty," I said. "Why'd you bring me here?"

"Because Komaki's coming."

"What?"

She nodded, either grimly or wearily. "You've known that."

"I didn't expect it so soon."

"Naiji just told me, maybe half an hour ago."

"How many soldiers?"

"We still don't know. Perhaps sixty, perhaps six hundred."

I smiled at that. "Your scouts can't count? Or is this a seer's report? If Dovriex sampled some bad mushrooms and dreamed—"

"Our scouts are birds, Rifkin. They understand *a few* and *a lot*. That's all."

"Oh."

"Want a tour of the defenses?"

"I've done a little looking on my own."

"You don't say." She indicated the cliff with a jerk of her chin. "We're fairly safe here."

"They can't get above us?"

"Not even if they were goats."

"What if they were mountaineers?"

"If you're trying to say the Spirits may have come this way, I know that already. I'll leave a few youths here with an elder who knows about war. They can shout for help if they need it."

I nodded. "Sounds reasonable."

The southeast wall grew out of the mountain, thirty feet above a narrow lip. Beyond that was a sheer drop for far too many feet. This was the route Naiji and I had taken the night before, climbing endlessly up a knotted line. My arms ached to remember it.

"This is probably our safest post. We'll only need a guard or two up here," Feschian said, looking down to where Avarineo watched. "And that's only in case they learn to fly."

I thought she was making a joke. Then I remembered that the Spirits were willing to employ witches to battle witches. Komaki might too.

"Avarineo would be better used elsewhere."

"I know. I thought Livifal and Sivifal could take turns on this wall."

"Livifal and Sivifal?"

"The twins. Dovriex's sisters."

"Ah."

The southwest wall looked over most of the valley. The old trading road was visible in a few places as a dark line cutting through the trees. The ground sloped steeply up to the wall, so that a soldier would have to scramble on all fours through brush and loose rock. It would not be easy for armored warriors to climb with scaling ladders on their backs and a fusillade of arrows about their heads, but it could be done if they were determined.

"Half our force will be along this wall," Feschian said.

"Half," I repeated, counting them in my mind.

"Yes."

"Does that include the hearth cat?"

She did not smile. "Probably."

The main gate stood in the middle of the northeast wall, which was the shortest wall of the four. A moat had been carved centuries ago, and a trickle of water flowed through it from the melting snows. Splashing through knee-deep ice water might slow a few soldiers, but it would not stop them. The gate itself showed a few signs of rot. I wondered if Komaki had sufficient funds for cannon. That he could afford to hire a band of Spirits told me he was not poor.

"We'll put the rest here," Feschian said.

"How many's that? Four warriors and a couple of well-meaning farmers?"

"And several children."

"Oh, of course. How could I forget the children?"

"They can help. They'll bring weapons, deliver messages—"

"I know," I said. I sat on the parapet and stared out at the sunset. "What's our store of arrows?"

"Two or three hundred."

"Steel-tipped?"

"A few. Mostly bronze or fire-hardened."

"Will Talivane's trick with the lightning help us?"

"For a little while. But when he exhausts his power..." Feschian shrugged.

"How many could he kill before that happens?"

"Ten. Maybe twelve."

"Any of the rest of you have any helpful surprises?"

"A few. Nothing to count on, especially if Komaki's force is large. Magic is very tiring, and several successive spells would leave most of us too exhausted to do anything more. Best to plan to wage this battle conventionally."

I nodded. "Any secret weapons you've yet to tell me of? An alliance with giant mountain lizards? An army of the undead? A cache of slingshots?"

"Two slingshots."

"Great."

"There's an old musket in the armory. It might still fire."

"I'm overjoyed." I looked around. The walls were dotted with piles of rocks and wood, ready to be dumped on attackers below. While I looked, two witches came with buckets to the central well, so I knew they were stocking up on water in case Komaki's force breached the walls and we had to retreat to the central keep. Feschian was obviously competent; I doubted there was anything she had overlooked.

"You've sent out hunters?"

"Yes. Two archers and a falconer, and several herbalists, as well."

"How long could we stand a siege?"

"Three weeks, maybe four."

"Eating how often?"

"Once a day, very little."

I thought about this. "What about your Queen? Can we hope for her help?"

"Of course. Hope is free."

"Oh."

"Well? Any suggestions?"

"One. Surrender."

"Komaki's often said he'd never allow a witch to live."

I looked at her. "I understand why Talivane wants to stay. He's trapped by his pride. What excuse do the rest of you have?"

"Loyalty."

"Stupidity."

"No, Rifkin. You've only seen one side of Talivane's nature. He can be kind. He gave us all homes when we had none."

"Is a home worth a life?"

She raised an eyebrow. "If you're so wise, why do you stay here?"

I looked away, and we walked to the dining hall in silence. Talivane nodded to us from his seat. Feschian told him, "I showed Rifkin the walls."

"Good," he said.

Naiji smiled at me. "What did you think?"

"A great view," I said. "You should open a resort for the wealthy."

Talivane laughed. "A little late for that, I fear."

Kivakali sat beside her husband. She never looked up at me.

Dinner consisted of more bear stew. I ate my share without regrets. If there are gods who judge us, surely they think it appropriate that the bear, dying while trying to take my life, now helped to sustain it. Most people ate with gusto, which told me that Komaki's advance was not yet common news.

Avarineo sat glumly, eating raw tubers. I caught his glance once, and he looked away. Perhaps he still wanted vengeance on me for the bear's death. This afternoon's demonstration might only have convinced him to be subtle when he finally attacked me. I wondered what Avarineo would consider subtle. I decided that if we were both standing near a cliff and the giant suddenly shouted, "Look! Magrath's comet!" I would not look.

I was wiping the last bits of stew from my bowl with a crust of flatbread when Talivane stood. The hall quieted, except for a few infants. Talivane said, "I have news for you all. Komaki is coming."

Several people stood in anger or fear. Talivane raised his open hands and smiled soothingly. "He's not here yet. We have until tomorrow, at least."

"How do you know?" asked one of the red-haired twins, Livifal or Sivifal.

Talivane turned to the scarred fencer. He said, "I spoke with a hawk."

The other twin said, "Which?"

"Old Firewing."

Both twins nodded. One said, "Probably true, then. Stardart couldn't tell the difference between a merchant's wagon and a cannon on wheels, and all Young Firewing remembers are mice and hares. Old Firewing can be trusted."

The fencer smiled patiently. "That's what I thought."

"How far away are they?" asked Dovriex.

"Ten miles, maybe fifteen," Naiji said.

"I expect them tomorrow afternoon," Talivane stated. "So we have until then to prepare. Perhaps longer. If they arrive late, they may not attack until the following morning."

The plump shape-changer stood. "I've thought about this. We should attack them first." He spoke with determination, then looked around for approval. Avarineo pounded his fist on the table in agreement. I wondered if these two were friends.

"Oh?" Talivane turned to him. "How?"

"I could go and have a look-see. Might learn something."

"And you might not."

"Might kill a few." He grinned.

"The risk isn't worth it." Talivane smiled at the man. "We'll need you here, Fat Cat."

Dovriex said, "They keep too much steel around them to try for a sending."

Talivane nodded. "I suspect there's nothing we can do tonight."

"What about your hawks?" I asked. "How well can you control them?" Everyone stared at me as if I'd materialized among them at that instant. "Just asking," I said.

"We control them well," said Talivane. "Why?"

I hesitated because I seemed to be the only one aware that we made our plans to defeat Komaki in the presence of his daughter. Kivakali continued to sit passively, so I said, "Could they carry tins of hot coal to drop on the Duke's tents?"

Talivane stroked his lip with his index finger. "Interesting." He glanced at Naiji.

She shook her head. "Not the hawks. Not in the dark, anyway. And tin would get too hot for their talons. And the camp's too far for them to fly burdened."

I shrugged. "How am I doing in the stupidest question of the night contest?"

Naiji smiled. "You haven't won yet, Rifkin. The owls may be able to help us. We could put the coals into clay pots with handles of twine. The owls might be able to carry them comfortably."

Talivane said, "Any other suggestions, Rifkin?"

"What other animals do you control?"

Naiji said, "We don't control any, as you think of it. We speak with them."

"Mindspeaking?"

"Something like that. Iron Eyes there is our falconer." She tipped her head toward the thin fencer. "But Livifal's better at talking with the birds. Sivifal's talents are with fish. Avarineo speaks with most animals, but Feschian is good with small ones. And Talivane has an affinity with snakes and lizards."

"I should have guessed that."

Talivane smiled. "Annoy me more, Rifkin, and you would do well to search your bed for my friends before you lie in it."

I kept myself from offering a retort concerning Naiji.

Naiji said, "Why do you want to know these things?"

"They may be useful. Could you arrange for an army of, say, moose and bear and forest cat and such to battle Komaki?"

Naiji shook her head. "We communicate with many beasts,

but we can only command a few. Most animals know enough to fear armed warriors in large numbers."

"Any other suggestions?" Talivane asked.

I nodded. "I gave one to your captain, but she didn't like it."

"What was it?"

"Surrender. But from what I hear about Komaki, abandoning this castle might be the better idea."

He squinted at me. "You don't think we can defend it?"

"It's possible."

"Then we'll do it."

"Swimming from Land's End to Palm Isle in winter is also possible," I said. "Still, no one's managed to do it."

"If we run from Komaki, our cause will mean nothing."

"Neither will your lives, if you don't."

"Oh? And where would we go if we left, Rifkin? Who would take us in?" He hesitated, and I started to speak, but he said, "Don't tell me again of Witchhold if you can't lead us to it." He glanced around. "Anyone have any intelligent suggestions?"

No one spoke. I glanced at Kivakali and saw that she stared at me. The moment our eyes met, she looked away. I thought I saw tension in her face, though I might not have. I might have only seen what I expected to see. Perhaps she was only a little drunk and very weary of plans in which she would take no part.

"There's much that should be done," Feschian announced. "We'll divide into smaller groups and work late."

I chose Dovriex's crew and sliced thin strips of venison for most of the night. When the smoking racks were full and the hickory fires burned properly beneath them, I staggered off for a much-desired sleep.

⚓ 13 ⚓

CASTLE GROMANDIEL

THE SCREAM THAT woke me during my second night in Castle Gromandiel was higher and shriller than the one I'd heard the night before. Stories are told in Loh about the girl who cried "Shark!" and I admit that a nagging feeling I had done all this before kept me from hurrying as much as I might have. I grabbed my cloak as well as my short sword and only tried the connecting door to Naiji's room once before I hurried into the hall. My first call was "Lady Naiji!" After listening for a second or two, my second was "Feschian!"

I heard light, quick footsteps, and then the captain's voice. "Perhaps we should give you a schedule of the events of the day, Rifkin."

"It'd be amusing to see. Dinner at dusk, conversation until nine, and don't miss everyone's favorite, the midnight death shrieks at, ah . . ."

"Yes?"

"Midnight," I finished lamely. "Naiji's well?"

"Yes."

"Why don't you tell me what's happening? It'd make life easier for both of us."

"You needn't know."

I heard something harsh, possibly annoyance, perhaps disapproval, in her voice. I said, "And you needn't either?"

I listened to the silent hallway until she said "No."

"What do you think they're doing?"

"You tell me, Rifkin."

I bit my lip as I thought, then said, "It's sorcery, probably. Involving the Spirits, almost certainly. I assume that if anyone asks, we'll hear that another one died during questioning?"

"Probably."

I thought of the quality of the shriek and guessed, "The girl?"

"Yes."

I remembered her, sneering at us in the dungeon. I hoped her end was quick. And then I pitied her companion more, the fearful boy who still waited. Would he follow tomorrow evening? Or would Chifeo take his place?

"Why's Talivane doing this?"

"Why does he do anything? To help our cause, I'm sure."

"You've no sympathy for the Spirits?" I said, not expecting any.

"No. But that doesn't mean I like this. I hope Talivane learns all he needs, soon."

"So do I. Will this happen again tomorrow at midnight?"

"I don't know," Feschian said, and I wished for enough light to see her face. A thought flashed through my mind. *Not with so much iron near,* and left as quickly.

"What is it?" Feschian's voice was quick and suspicious.

"Nothing," I said, perhaps too fast, trying to hide my fear. I knew, in that moment, who had struck down Mondivinaw, and why.

"You're sure?"

I made myself smile, for I assumed that she watched me with witchsight. "Of course." I lie fairly well when I must.

"Whatever you say, Rifkin."

"Did you learn anything more about Kivakali?" I asked.

"No. You?"

"No. Watch Naiji, watch Kivakali, and try to save this castle.

I doubt it's possible to do one of those things well, let alone all three."

"Probably not. Go sleep, Rifkin. You have your class to give in the morning, and archery's been added to the schedule."

"It has? Thanks for telling me."

"Think nothing of it. I've been trying to tell you many things. It's nice that one's gotten through." She patted my arm to say the insult was not meant, then left me.

I returned calmly enough to my room and put aside my cloak and sword. What I wanted was a skin or two of wine, but I doubted I could find the kitchen or the cellar in the dark. I didn't want to wander near Talivane's quarters, not even by accident. I was not afraid of being found. I was afraid of what I would find, and what it would mean to my vow to Naiji. I had enough worries already. I did not need to go looking for more.

I shoved the pallet against the wall, then stood nude at the center of the small room. I began to walk the first pattern of the Art, transforming each ugly killing technique into a dancer's action, or at least trying. The second pattern was more difficult, which pleased me, and I moved faster, striking harder. By the time I'd finished the third, I was racing. I executed each action with twice the strength that was needed, and three times the speed. My teachers would have been furious.

I made myself see opponents at each end of each part of the fourth pattern, so the move called "heron takes flight" ripped three ribs from Talivane's side, and the one called "cat scratches" tore Izla Seaprince's testicles from his body. "Dragon leaps" needed someone, so I set a faceless Spirit there, but as my foot almost tore his head from his neck, he suddenly had a face, the face of the girl Spirit who had died this evening. That made me stumble, which was never a part of the fourth pattern. I had the choice of crying or continuing, so I continued, from fifth to sixth to seventh. . . .

"Rifkin?" Naiji's voice came from the hall. "What're you doing in there?" Her tone was gentle, curious, slightly guarded.

"What's Komaki look like?"

"He's short and thin and balding. Why?"

"Not tall and fat?"

"No."

"Maybe he has a henchman who looks like that?"

"Maybe."

"Good. I just killed his henchman seven times. The last time was particularly thorough. I popped his eyes out like grapes."

"What?"

"Nothing."

"Rifkin?"

"Yes."

"May I come in?"

"Sure."

I felt a caress of cool air as the door to my room opened and closed, but I did not bother to look. I took a deep breath and began the ninth pattern. I did it for Naiji, not for myself, and the anger and fear left me. My limbs moved by themselves, calmly and slowly and strongly. My arms swept the air as if I flew instead of killed, and my legs and body seemed to step and leap through high grass. I forgot my imaginary opponents, forgot my real ones, forgot the sudden, hated knowledge of the intruder who spoke in my skull, forgot even that Naiji was there until I finished the pattern.

"Rifkin?"

I came out of the final posture, and though my mind left the pattern behind, I was calmer than before. Enough of myself had returned to me to expect a compliment from Naiji, for the part of me that watched saw how very well that last pattern had gone. I said, "Yes?"

"Hold me." Her voice broke with the second word, and I staggered backward as she threw herself into my arms.

"Whoa!" I said. "There, now." She was crying, so I stroked her head with one hand while I hugged her. "There, now," I repeated, and I remembered why I had walked the patterns at midnight. "It's all right," I said, which I suspected was a lie, but that did not matter then.

"Love me," she said.

"I don't—"

"No!" She forced her lips against mine with sudden violence, and her tongue tried to force its way into my mouth.

I cupped her head with both hands and pushed her back. "You don't have to—"

"Love me!" she said. "Love me, Rifkin, damn you!" Her hand clutched my little man as if she would force him to stand.

"Naiji," I said.

"Lady Naiji!" she corrected. "Lady Naiji!"

What could I do? I could not calm her and I could not please her then. I caught her wrist and hoped she would not treat me as I'd imagined myself treating the Seaprince some twenty minutes earlier. "Lady Naiji," I whispered. "Help me."

"Help you?" Her voice was scornful.

"Yes. Help me."

"Help..." Her grip loosened, and she said, "Gods, Rifkin, I—"

I stroked her hair again. "Quiet, Lady. We've both experienced much this evening, I suspect."

She stiffened. "You do?"

"Yes."

"What've you learned?"

"That someone else lives in my skull. What've you learned?"

She laughed. "Oh, Rifkin..." She relaxed in my arms and began to stroke me too. "Later, Rifkin. Ask me later, please?"

"Certainly, Lady. Whatever you wish."

"How did you learn?"

"About the other? Remember when your father fell?"

I felt her chin nodding against me. "Yes," she said.

"That wasn't me. It was someone else in my mind."

"No, Rifkin. Not someone else in your mind. Another mind in your skull."

"I know. I figured that—" I stared at her. "How much do you know?"

"Shush." She hugged me. "Calm yourself." Her voice became almost bitter, almost self-mocking. "There's no knowledge too terrible to bear."

"How much?" I repeated, not caring for anything then but an answer.

"That there are two minds in your body, Rifkin. Which belongs and which is the intruder, I can't tell. Whose the other's is, I don't know. But I can guess."

"Yes?"

"Yes." She squeezed me again. "This body belongs to a witch, and you aren't one."

The night seemed colder then. I moved away from her to spread my sleeping pallet and then to wrap myself in a blanket.

She watched without speaking. At last, I said, "When did you guess?"

"I didn't guess, Rifkin. I told you I looked into your skull when I healed you in the woods. I learned more than I told you."

"What else?"

"That's all."

"Really?"

"Yes."

I studied her. "I wish I could tell truth as you do."

She laughed. "No, you don't. Will you share your blanket?"

"You're warm enough in your clothes."

"That can be remedied." She began to undress.

"Why do you trust me?"

"Because you're honest, Rifkin."

"And the other? Do you trust him too?"

"Not at all."

"I lied this afternoon. I, Rifkin Truthteller."

"Oh?"

"To the Spirits."

"So? What's a lie told to liars?"

"A lie."

"Oh. What did you say?"

"I told one I would kill him."

"And you didn't? I'd think you'd be proud of that."

"You weren't there."

"No." She was naked now. "You'll share?" I opened the blanket, and she hurried in. "Thanks." She pressed herself against me. A hand began to caress my thigh.

"No," I said.

"You're strange, Rifkin."

I glanced at her. "Me? Old Rifkin Twominds? What makes you say that?"

"And you can joke any time?"

"Not always well. I'm sorry."

"You shouldn't worry about the other."

I had to think a moment to know whom she meant. "No?"

"No. It may be his body, but you control it."

"I thought he was dead."

She nodded.

"He wants it back," I said.

"How do you know that?"

"I don't. But he never spoke before. He must want it back."

"How long have you had—"

"This body?"

"Yes."

"Two years. Almost three."

"And you still want it?"

"Yes."

"Then keep it, Rifkin."

"That might not be easy."

We lay there in silence for some time. I said, "Your turn, now. What did you learn this evening?"

"Not yet, Rifkin. If we're still alive tomorrow night, I'll tell you then."

"As you wish, Lady."

"Who is it?"

I started, thinking she had heard someone I had not, then understood. "Izla Seaprince," I said.

"That's the name Chifeo spoke."

"He was more accurate than I thought."

"Why did you deny it?"

"Because I'm Rifkin. Rifkin..." I searched for another name to identify myself, but I could not find a single one.

"Rifkin," Naiji agreed. She kissed my cheek.

"Not Izla," I said.

"No. Not Izla."

"How can I kill him?"

"I thought you never chose to kill."

"Is there a way?"

"I don't know, Rifkin. Talivane might."

"I don't want to be in Talivane's debt."

"You don't have to."

"No?"

"No. Just learn to live with Ixla."

"Izla," I corrected.

"Right. What's the story?"

"You'll tell Talivane?"

She said softly, "He doesn't need to know any of this."

"What if the other takes over?"

"From what I could sense of him, Talivane would prefer him to you."

That amused me in a morbid way. "Probably true."

"Well?"

"It's getting late," I said.

"So?"

"The short version, then."

"The long."

"Or none at all," I said.

"The short would be fine."

"There was once a prince and a bodyguard who changed bodies, planning to change back again. They never did."

She stared at me. "That's the story?"

"Enough of it, for now."

"What happened to your first body? Your . . . original body? Is it dead?"

"I don't know. It might be. Perhaps that's why Izla speaks inside me now."

"Aren't you curious?"

"Very."

"And?"

I turned away from her, as if I would go to sleep. "I don't know."

"You mentioned a son."

"He died, Naiji. I don't want to talk about it."

"Your original body may still be walking around, and you don't care?"

"I care very much. What can I do?"

"Go back. To Istviar."

I turned over to face her. "You saw Chifeo's reaction to me. Any Ladizhan I met would think I was Izla Seaprince. The Spirits pursue him with orders to kill him. They have good reason to do so. All I can do is flee."

"To here?" Naiji began to laugh.

"Stop," I said.

"Sorry. But of all the places you could come—"

"I thought it was coincidence at first, Lady. But if Izla is awake in my skull, he may have directed me. Magic seems to make him stronger. At least, he never spoke before, that I noticed."

"And now?"

"Twice. Once when your father fell. Again tonight." I suddenly remembered the sensation of being watched while Naiji healed me in the woods. I wanted to curse her for waking him then, but I realized that I would have died if she had done nothing.

"And you never recognized him."

"No. I thought he was dead. Two minds in one skull..." I closed my eyes. "It never occurred to me."

She laughed. "A number of things never occurred to you, Rifkin. You wear a witch's body. You should learn to use it."

I brought my hand up the inside of her thigh. "I have."

She giggled and caught my wrist. "Not like that. As a witch."

"I'm not one." I turned to move my other hand along her side.

"You are, Rifkin," she said patiently. "You are. That's why I brought you here. I'd never have trusted some magicless human the way I trust you."

"But I'm—"

"Magic is in your body and your blood, Rifkin. Don't ever allow yourself to be tested with iron like you did this afternoon. It was only your ignorance and your disbelief that saved you."

"I'm Rifkin," I said. "Not a witch."

"You want to stay Rifkin and not become Izla Whatzis?"

"Yes," I whispered.

"Learn to use your magic, then. I suspect it's the only way." She lay there, holding me. "Well?"

"Maybe."

"I don't lie to you now."

"I know."

"I could teach you."

I swallowed, then said, "Do so."

"You're frightened?" she asked in surprise.

"A little."

"A lot. Poor Rifkin." She wiped sweat from my forehead. "Relax. Izla won't destroy you while you sleep, nor will Rifkin Justanotherhuman become a wizard tonight. The little tricks take months to master, and the art of magic requires years. I'm not about to begin teaching you now."

"Good."

"But you should learn."

"I will."

She stroked my brow, then kissed it softly. "If I can help you escape Izla, I will."

"Thank you."

"I like you, Rifkin."

"Doesn't everyone?"

"No, Rifkin," she said patiently. "But I like you."

"That means you're thinking of the things we could do together?"

"No. It just means I like you." She squeezed me. "Go to sleep."

I closed my eyes and began to concentrate on my breathing, as though I planned to meditate. That usually let me sleep almost as soon as I lay down, but too many thoughts kept peeking into my mind. I almost whispered "Good night, Izla," just to show myself that I could still joke in the face of danger, a talent many fools pride themselves on. The thought that he might answer kept me quiet.

After a bit I remembered what Naiji had said about being willing to couch with a boundman, but never willing to sleep with one. I said her name quietly as I started to ask when she would leave me. A faint snore was her answer.

≫ 14 ≪

ISTVIAR

KIYAN OF ISTVIAR gave me a post in her mother's guards. We were secret lovers, or so we thought, though many people would smile when I would leave the barracks to spend an evening out, or when Kiyan would have me attend her for an afternoon of personal instruction. My two years in the City of Ships were happy ones. I became an instructor of sorts, teaching the palace guards what I knew of the Warrior-Saint's Art and learning other techniques from those who knew them. When Kiyan's mother died and she became the Sea Queen, she sent for me. We met in Kiyan's bedroom. When I moved to kiss her, she held up her hand between us, offering a heavy coin purse without comment or expression.

"What's this?" I asked, taking it.

"Your pay."

"Ah."

"I'm going to marry."

"And this isn't a dowry."

She smiled and caressed my cheek. "No, Rifkin. I've decided to marry one of the western princes. It's for the good of Istviar. It'll strengthen the Alliance."

"Ah. For the good of Istviar. I understand."

"I still care for you, Rifkin. I might be tempted to keep you here if I didn't."

"Which means I must leave?"

She nodded. "I don't expect him to keep a lover, Rifkin. I can hardly keep you."

I nodded slowly.

"I have met him. He seems kind."

"I'm glad of that."

"Really?"

"No," I said. "Well, yes. Maybe."

She laughed and beckoned to me. "One last time, old friend?"

I swallowed carefully, set the bag of coins aside, and said, "Of course."

In the morning, lying in her sheets, I tried to memorize her features and wondered whether I loved Kiyan or only what she represented to me. She woke, snuggled against me, and said, "I'll miss you."

"Good."

She must have heard some bitterness in my voice. Her eyes opened and she studied me, completely awake. "Rifkin. If I send for you, will you come to me?"

"Though ten thousand soldiers should bar the way."

She laughed and put her head against my neck. "What a dope."

I returned to Loh. I was older, and I was rich, and I had served the Sea Queen. I discovered that the Searich line did not despise me, and that little Rileel, one of Vayil's sisters who had been widowed the year before, was much more attractive than I remembered. Rileel and I lived together for nineteen years. Vayil and Svanik both came to Loh to visit, and we even practiced the Art together, and I was content.

News traveled slowly between Istviar and Loh, but we heard of Kiyan's marriage, and later, that it resulted in a son. Kiyan's rule seemed to be a good one, though people muttered that she was too kind to Istviar's witches. She decreased the witches' taxes and no longer required them to inhabit Istviar's witches' quarter. Still, Istviar prospered under her rule, and I knew of no serious discontent in the Sea Queen's country.

The Searich family grew richer while I lived with them. We bought a fourth boat. When Istviar established a garrison in Loh, I arranged a contract with the garrison's leader to supply them with fish. Rileel and I had four children—a son by her first marriage, then twin daughters, then a son. When Kiyan's messenger came—

I write this too quickly. I can already hear the complaints of my favorite critic. Very well, I'll tell more of my later life in Loh.

When I was one of Tchanin's students, Rileel was a gawky girl who thought she loved me, and I had little time for her. I never saw her for what she was; I saw her for what she was not. She was not her older sister, and she was not Kiyan. I knew her flaws very well: she laughed too loudly, and she giggled at the most simplistic jokes. Others in Tchanin's class had noticed the looks that Vayil's sister gave me. They kidded me about her. She embarrassed me, and I was Second Student, who deserved far better than Vayil's silly sister.

When I returned to Loh, Rileel was a widowed mother who bore her sorrow well. I was rich, and I had bought a hut and a small boat. For the first week I spent my days in the boat, trying to learn what the smallest children of the fishing families already knew. I spent my evenings sober, but in the second week, I passed two evenings quite drunk on happiness milk. When I woke the third morning of the second week, Rileel was waiting in the yard outside my hut. I knotted a sheet like a sarong about my waist. "'Leel. Mornin'."

"You need a helper in your boat," she said quietly, not meeting my eyes.

I nodded.

"All of my family know these waters."

"I know."

"My lover's boat was caught in a storm when he was too far out."

"I heard."

"I was too pregnant to be with him."

"He shouldn't have gone out too far."

"If I'd been with him, he wouldn't have." She looked up, and her eyes, I noticed, were a very common brown, but that brown was no less attractive for being common. "If you take me as a helper, I'll only ask a quarter of your catch. And I'll double that catch."

"Great," I said. "That guarantees two fish today." When she smiled slightly, I said, "You could work on one of your family's boats."

She didn't answer. I thought of Vayil's independence, and realized that it was a trait of the Searich family.

"No matter, Rileel. You're ready to go?"

"My mother is caring for my son. I'm ready."

We caught more fish that day than I had caught all week.

Rileel moved into my hut seven months after that day. Our daughters were born almost a year later, and our son, ten months after them. And now I will tell the next part much too quickly, and I will make no apology. We had eighteen good years in Loh. I continued to practice the Art, even though I knew that I loved my family and my village too much to seek spiritual transcendence. I taught what I could to my children. In the nineteenth year plague came to Loh, and I watched my family die.

I do not know why the plague never touched me. I had been very sick for a week in Istviar; perhaps that satisfied the spirits of illness. I only know that in that spring, a trading ship came to Loh from a western city. A week later people began to sicken. Sores developed in their mouths, their groins, their armpits. They screamed. They soiled themselves like babies. They become unconscious. They died. One-fourth of Loh's people died in three weeks.

When I had buried the last of my family—my eldest son, Rileel's firstborn—I went to the man who made happiness milk and gave him a fistful of coins. "Bring a jug every morning to my hut. Tell me when I need to pay you again. I have more coins."

"Yes, Rifkin Searich."

I stared at him until he said, "What did I say? I didn't mean—"

I tapped myself. "Rifkin Freeman."

"Of course."

"A jug every morning," I repeated. "And when you want more coins, I'll dig up more for you. Amazing, isn't it? Gold doesn't rot in the earth."

When he said nothing, I returned to my hut. I tried very hard to stay drunk after that, but after several days, I shattered that day's jug and began to practice the Art again. I may have practiced for an hour or so every day while my family lived, but when they died, I practiced all day. I remembered enough of what I had learned on the White Mountain, and I set myself new tests. One day three months later, as I did the Thirteenth Pattern—the longest and most difficult—in reverse at one-fourth its normal speed, I became aware of a black-garbed figure watching me.

I finished without altering my speed. I did the final bow to my watcher, who nodded in approval. He was a small, dark man with his hair cut close to his skull. He returned my bow and laughed. "I heard that a madman lived in Loh who was a greater follower of the Warrior-Saint's Art than any Priest or Spirit who ever lived."

"You hear exaggerations."

"So I see." His clothes were more closely tailored than those of a Priest. He could only be a Spirit. When my family lived, his presence would have frightened or angered me. "Still, you're very good."

I sat to begin meditating.

"Come to Moon Isle. We'll have a place for you."

I let my lids half close.

"You cannot want gold, or you would not live like this. So I won't offer gold to you."

I listened to my breath, thinking of inhaling deeply and letting my exhalation come when it would.

"However, I can give you a purpose, Rifkin Madman."

I thought I did not react, but he laughed.

"There's evil in Istviar. Humanity is threatened. It's time to finish what the Warrior-Saint began."

"Go away."

He laughed again. "The witches live among us, Rifkin. They hold places of trust in our government. They establish a reign that will be far harder to overthrow than the Witches' Empire. They'll control us from places of political and economic power. They'll rule the world if we don't stop them."

"Fine," I said. "Let them."

"Remember me," he said, and he left.

Svanik Priest came five or six days later. His face was much smoother than it had been when he was a child. Now, more lines showed on the side that had never been burned. He came while I was practicing my leaping side kicks. "You don't have to stay here," he said at last.

I remembered that speaking to the Spirit had not helped, so I continued my kicks. From a tree I'd hung a bag of dirt that served as a target.

"There's a place for you on the White Mountain."

I kicked.

"You aren't what you were, Rifkin. You were only concerned for yourself then. You've learned to love—"

I kicked again, and I had not thought I could kick harder than I had kicked before. I could.

"We all grieve with you. Vayil is at her mother's now. We would have come sooner—"

I switched to leaping front kicks.

"We didn't know, Rifkin. We rarely have messengers."

I could do double front kicks before landing, though that called for judging the spinning of the bag between the first and second kicks.

"I loved Rileel, too, you—"

I spun as I landed from the last kick and said, "If you don't want to learn whether I am still Second Student and you are still Third, leave now."

He pursed his lips as though to speak, then nodded and left.

When Vayil came that afternoon, I faced her in fighting stance. She opened her arms wide to show she was defenseless. "Rifkin."

I could not speak in sentences for fear of crying or attacking her. "Go. Away. Now."

She nodded to me and went.

Someone brought food and water every day. Only later did I realize that it was the man I had paid to bring me happiness milk. I practiced and I meditated, but my meditation was a flight from thought and responsibility. It did not bring me peace. When I dreamed, the Black Shark chased my family, gnawing upon them while I could do nothing. Sometimes the White Lady appeared, and she would entice my family aboard her ship. They went trusting her. When they had boarded, the White Lady's ship moved away as though a strong wind had caught its sails. Its masts were as bare as oak trees in winter. I screamed from the shore for the White Lady to return, to release my family or to take me also. She only smiled at me. Her smile said that I had conspired with her in my family's death.

My last visitor was a boy in the vest and helmet of Kiyan's guard. He came almost a month after Svanik and Vayil had returned to Loh. He said, "The Sea Queen asks you to come to Istviar."

I nodded. "Lead me."

Kiyan received me in the small room where we had often met. She wore a red and white silk sarong that I had admired, and her hair was tied back as if she were a student again with Tchanin. She smiled gently, and for a moment, it was as though I were returning again from the White Mountain and she was there to comfort me. "Hello, old friend." Her voice was weak, and lower than I remembered."

"Kiyan." I nodded to her.

"I've heard. I'm sorry."

I nodded again.

"I remember Rileel. I hope you treated her better than you did when we were students."

"A little."

"Good." She clapped her hands, and the curtain to the room was brushed aside by a small, dark young man in loose silk trousers and silver jewelry on his fingers, arms, ankles, and ears. He smiled a secretive, superior smile as Kiyan said, "My son, Izla of Istviar."

Izla assessed me with his glance. "This is the peasant who was your . . . friend, Mother?"

"This is Rifkin Artist, Izla."

"Artist?" Izla laughed. "One of those fellows who break trees with their foreheads and fight bulls on feast days? He must be very proud. There aren't many who are the equals of trees."

Kiyan's eyes closed for a moment. "My son is a fool, Rifkin. That is why I've asked you to come here."

"To teach him?" I asked.

Izla laughed delightedly.

"No," Kiyan answered. "To protect him."

We stood in the room in silence. If Izla had laughed, I might have left then. He gnawed at the cuticle of the little finger of his left hand. My youngest son at Loh had done exactly that when he was nervous or thinking of distant things. "Very well," I said. "I'll protect him. From what?"

"Assassins. Rebellion. His own foolishness."

"I can't guarantee to save him from any of those."

"I know that." There was relief in Kiyan's voice, and that pleased me.

"I don't like this," Izla said.

"Poor baby," Kiyan answered.

"I can protect myself," Izla said, and his hands were suddenly encased in globes of fire.

"Fool!" Kiyan snapped her hand at him. A gust of wind extinguished Izla's flame.

I stared at them both. In songs, heroes wonder at such times if they have gone mad, but I did not disbelieve what I had seen. "Witches," I said.

Izla smiled. "He is quick, for a peasant."

"You see why my son needs protection?"

I touched my tongue to my lip, then nodded.

"The people whisper that Istviar is ruled by witches," Kiyan said. "And they are right. It's been a secret since the Witches' Empire fell. I'm not sure how the rumor began." She looked at Izla.

"I wasn't careless!"

"Maybe not." When she turned her eyes to me, she said with some pride, "Izla's the strongest witch in generations, Rifkin. In our family it's traditional to teach our children the truth about themselves when they reach their twentieth birthday, and then to begin instruction in using our art. Izla discovered his in puberty. One summer people in the palace began to feel as though they had no privacy, as if there were secret watchers hidden in the rooms. I discovered the truth one evening when I felt a clumsy spy in my mind and realized who it must be."

"I am tired of this story, Mother."

"Yes." She touched his shoulder kindly. "You may leave us now, if you wish."

"Good." He went without a farewell.

"Are you frightened of us, Rifkin?"

I nodded.

"I'm still Kiyan."

"I know."

"It doesn't change me."

"I know."

"You won't betray us?"

I shook my head slightly.

"Thank you." She closed her eyes, and I wondered if she were dismissing me. "He's not a bad son, Rifkin. I don't think so, anyway. I love him. But I didn't raise him well. Maybe I should have sent him to the Priests, just as my mother sent me. Izla's—" She opened her eyes. "He needs to learn about the world, but he might not have time."

"You mentioned rebellion."

"In the west. My consort's gone in hopes of quieting his people. Maybe he can do something. I don't know. I have agents among the people. They say the Warrior-Saint's Spirit will return to Istviar and cleanse the city."

"I've heard."

She swallowed. I saw then that she was close to tears. "Have I been a bad ruler? I try to help the witches and the humans, and it only gets worse, Rifkin. Why?"

I had no answer. After a moment or two she said "Go, Rifkin Guardian. Your old bunk is yours again." I shrugged and nodded and went.

For the next fourteen months we watched the Ladizhar Alliance crumble. Messengers came each week with news from the west, from the isles, from the east, from the inlands. In the latter part of the fall of Istviar, the messengers came several times a day. For the most part we carried on life in the Sea Queen's palace as best we could. Kiyan grew weaker as the strain increased. When the western provinces fell to the Spirits, the embargoes began. Kiyan walked each day through the streets of Istviar, greeting the people and promising that the shortages would end soon. It seemed that her family might have held Istviar, but on one of her walks a dark figure in a crowd threw a poisoned dart at her chest. The assassin escaped. When I learned the story, I doubted I could have saved her. I'll never know. I was protecting Izla.

Izla passed most of the week of his reign in the throne room. He had clerks bring him texts from the palace libraries during the day. At night he had parties there, inviting ambitious offspring of Istviar's wealthier families. It seemed there was always one who would accompany Izla to his chambers. His bed partners were never invited to subsequent parties, and all knew this. Perhaps they went with him because then they would not have to return. Perhaps each hoped to earn the Seaprince's love.

The evening before the City of Ships fell to the armies of the west, Izla led me to the libraries. "I could not save my mother," he said, "but I can save us, Rifkin. You still stand by the vow you swore?"

"Yes."

"Good." He threw a sheaf of old papers onto a desk and smoothed one with the flat of his hand. "Here!" He pointed at hieroglyphs I could not understand. The age of the paper made his following words seem more credible. "You're safe enough from the Spirits, Rifkin. They don't care about a bodyguard. But they know my face. They'll come with iron, and I don't know how to protect myself against them. But you do!" He laughed. "I need your permission, Rifkin. I can't force this. If you allow me, we will change bodies for a few weeks. I'll travel along the coast in your body and no one will know me. You'll go north, where no one knows Izla. In a week or two you'll have my body safely away from the Ladizhar. The spell will fade then, and you'll be free of your promise to my mother. Do you agree?"

I don't know if he truly expected me to deny him. I nodded, and the rest happened as he said. I woke in the room in Izla's body. My body had already gone. I took up my bodyguard's gear and fled.

For several months after that I went to sleep each evening expecting to wake somewhere along the coast. Each morning I woke a fugitive. So I came to Castle Gromandiel.

15

CASTLE
GROMANDIEL

NAIJI SAID "WAKE. It's almost dawn."

"Almost dawn. Right."

She nudged me with her elbow, and I said "Hey!"

She sighed. "I thought a Master Artist would wake instantly."

"I do."

"And fall asleep as quickly."

"True. Hey!" I scrambled against the wall to escape her tickling. "I'm awake, woman."

She grinned and walked into her room. I tried to decide if her buttocks usually swayed so nicely or if she was adding something extra for my benefit. "I'm very awake," I called after her. "Care to come back and see how much?"

"No, Rifkin. There's much for us to do today."

"I thought you ruled here."

"I do. That's why there's so much to do."

"Right." I saw no reason to wake fully, so I staggered through my morning habits, eventually becoming conscious in spite of

myself. Someone had taken yesterday's clothing and set out
baggy black pants and a jacket with silver trim. When I put
on the old brown boots and looked in the mirrored wall, I
considered asking if the blue and burgundy outfit was still
around. "Who's been choosing my clothes?" I called.

"Talivane's given you a few things that were his when he
was younger."

"Ah. I hope he dies soon. Painfully. In checked pants and
a striped shirt."

"Something's wrong?" She came into the bathroom, then
smiled. "You look like you're going to a dance."

"I'd like to. On Talivane."

"It doesn't matter. When all this ends, someone'll fix better
clothing for you."

"They won't follow Talivane's suggestions?"

"No."

"That'll be nice, then."

Naiji wore her hunting garb with a basket-hilted saber
sheathed on one hip and a heavy knife lashed to the other thigh.
I'd already transferred my collection of surprises to their hiding places, so I belted on my short sword, then picked up my
axe with my left hand. When long ago I took it from a fellow
who no longer needed it, it had a leather hood to cover its
head. After I had to hammer someone to death because the
hood was on, I threw the hood away. I ruined one pair of pants
by carrying the thing unsheathed, but I didn't bleed to death.
I was careful after that.

Naiji tapped the steel stars that decorated my old belt. "Say!
Are those throwing darts?"

I nodded.

She shook her head. "My, you are a sneaky one. Are you
carrying any other weapons I don't know about?"

I shrugged, a little embarrassed.

"And here I've been thinking you were just color-blind."

That almost made me tell her what I kept in the boots.

We went to the kitchens. Avarineo sat at a table and slurped
tea from a mug. "Morning, mistress," he said.

"Morning, old friend." Naiji rubbed his head like a dog's,
and he grinned.

"Morning, Avarineo," I said.

He squinted, then smiled suddenly and said, "Morning,

R-r-r-rifkin! I like you very, very much! You, R-r-rifkin, are Avarineo's friend!"

I reminded myself again not to stand near any cliffs in the giant's presence.

Dovriex came out from a door near the back of the kitchens. A grey smudge on his cheek suggested that he had been tending the smokehouse. "Good morning, Naiji, Rifkin! What would you like for breakfast?"

"Something vile," I suggested.

He nodded. "Well then, my lucky fellow, you've come to the right place."

"Hot mold in muddy water?"

"Better than that." He handed me a bowl, and I stared into it.

"This looks like what you served yesterday."

"Ah, but now it's had time to age."

"Not enough. It hasn't decayed."

"You haven't tasted it yet."

I took a bite. "You're right. It's decayed." Then I saw that Naiji snacked on flatbread and jam. "But—"

"The privileges of rank," Naiji said. "But I'm not cruel. Want to smell it?"

"You're too kind. I'll eat my scum."

"This is scum?" Avarineo said. "I like this scum!"

"Guess who'll get seconds," said Dovriex.

"Guess who could keep them down," I said.

Dovriex looked hurt. When Dovriex looked hurt, he scowled and rested his hand on the cleaver at his hip. I decided to be more considerate of his feelings in the future. I said, "Sorry. It's not bad, actually."

"You can have seconds, too, then," he said.

On the other hand if I insulted him thoroughly, my end would be quick, and almost painless. "We'll have to take care of Komaki soon," I said.

Naiji glanced at me.

"If the Duke doesn't kill us, these breakfasts will."

Dovriex only grinned, so I finished the gruel. I sat there, drinking a bitter root tea and scowling at Naiji while she ate her second piece of flatbread and jam. That only made her seem to enjoy her meal more, so I smiled. She smiled back at me, and Avarineo said, "Lovey faces. Uck. Makes me sick."

"Oh?" I said. "I didn't think anything could."

Dovriex said, "Thanks, Rifkin. Half-rations for you to-morrow morning."

"Promises, promises."

I drank more tea, and Naiji and I smiled at each other for a bit. Dovriex busied himself with washing pots. Avarineo said, "Anyone making lovey faces should make them at someone tall and strong and handsome, not at foolish little—"

I glanced at him.

"—people like there aren't any of around here, oh no, not like my good friend R-r-r-rifkin, oh no. He's not a foolish little person. And anyone who says so will answer to me! I think I'll go away now."

Avarineo left. A minute or two later, Naiji said, "I think we should—"

"Make sure none of Komaki's warriors have sneaked into my bedroom? I agree."

Naiji smiled. "That's silly."

"You're right. Let's check your bedroom instead."

"Rifkin."

"Oh, all—" I turned as one of the twins ran into the room. "Sivifal," I said.

"Livifal," Naiji corrected. "What is it?"

"Your father, Lady. He's awake. He asks for you."

"And Talivane?" Naiji asked.

"No, Lady. You and the southerner."

"Oh?" Naiji looked at me.

"Yes," Livifal said.

I shrugged. Naiji said, "Then we go. Tell Talivane that Da's awake."

"Yes, Lady."

We strode briskly from the kitchens to the infirmary. Naiji said, "Let me do the talking."

"Sure."

"What'll he expect?"

I shook my head. "I don't know. He probably heard Izla's voice, though maybe only I did."

"Well, don't worry about it."

"Of course not. What's the worst he can do to me?"

"Since you're wearing iron, little."

"Fine."

"He might use the fact that he's partially paralyzed to paralyze you. Then he'd have someone strip the iron from you so you could be tormented for a few days. And then he'd kill you. Da's like that."

"Oh."

She reached over and squeezed my arm. "I was just teasing."

"Mondivinaw's not like that?"

"Well, he is. Once he caught a poacher and kept her alive for weeks by feeding her bits of her flesh. But I won't let him do anything to you."

"Thanks." I walked the rest of the way thinking that I had lived a full and interesting life, and that while I had expected to end it in many places, I had never expected to die while visiting an old man's sickbed. Telling myself that death now would end the threat of facing another of Dovriex's breakfasts did little to soothe me.

One of the twins met us outside Mondivinaw's door. "Sivifal?" I said.

The redhead nodded, then stepped back so Naiji could enter. There was a long moment of silence until Naiji called, "Rifkin! Come in!"

I entered and bowed to Mondivinaw. He had been propped up with several pillows, but I did not think he looked well. His left side was dead; his right was frantic. His bloodshot right eye twitched furiously, and he gestured like an epileptic with his arthritic right hand. "Lord," I said.

Naiji smiled slightly. "My father says..." She paused with an actor's sense of drama, or else a torturer's. "...that he hopes the great lord will forgive his presumptions."

Confused, I frowned, and Mondivinaw's twitchings grew worse. Naiji added with veiled amusement, "My father says he is physically incapable of abasing himself, though he would if he could, and that he knows too little of subservience to speak as humbly as he should. He hopes..." Her eyes flicked to Mondivinaw, then back to me. "...no, prays that the great lord understands and accepts this."

The old man's living eye seemed to plead with me. That told me Naiji's words were not some cruel whim of her own. I nodded numbly at the old man. I tried to swallow, thinking to speak, but my throat was dry.

Naiji said, "My father is infinitely grateful that the great lord—"

I shook my head.

Her voice began to mirror some of her father's concern. "He hopes he has not offended—"

"No," I said gruffly, wanting to leave. "He has not."

"He says the great lord should consider this castle his own."

"Lady—" I began.

"He says we will all serve the great lord as best we can."

"Naiji!" I said. "Damn it, I'm no great lord!"

Her eyes went suddenly wide in true surprise.

"Nor can I play one," I added.

She shook her head. "Rifkin, he knows that. He wasn't talking to you."

"To..." I looked from father to daughter.

"Yes," said Naiji.

After a long moment I said, "Tell him..." I searched for a way to say what I felt, and I thought about what sort of man this old witch must be, and I thought about his son, and I thought about Izla.

"Da hears, Rifkin. He just doesn't speak."

"I know that, damn it!" I crossed to his bed in two steps. "Listen, you..." The fear in his eye made me gentler, but not much. "Old man, I wish to help you and your family. Not for your sake. And any gods that may be, know it's not for Talivane's sake, either. But I wish to help you. I, Rifkin Boundman, not the wizard who lives in my head. And I will help you, if you don't oppose me. But if you do, I'll unleash him, understand me? I'll unleash him and he'll make every agony you've ever endured seem like pure bliss. Understand me? Damn you, understand me!"

Naiji grabbed my shoulder. "He understands, Rifkin!"

"Great lord," I sneered, glaring at her. She drew her hand back. "Great lord, my callused ass! I served that spoiled child for two—" I saw that her fear almost equaled her father's. "Forget it," I said. "Just forget it." I stalked out, and as I went, Izla whispered *Well done*.

"Shut up!" I cried. Both of the twins were in the hall, and they glanced at me as if they expected madness from southerners but wished it came as a quieter, more discreet insanity.

I picked a hall and walked. Someone followed me. I turned at random, and my follower turned, too, then we both took a flight of very dusty stairs. At the top I told myself that I had been indulgent enough for a lifetime or two, perhaps I should play at intelligence for a minute. I had believed this was Naiji coming to comfort or confront me, but if it was an assassin instead, I would feel very stupid in the moment before I died.

It was Naiji. She stopped midway up the stairs and said, "Well?"

"It's all right."

"He's an old man."

"He's a vicious, stupid, and cowardly old fool. I've known a thousand like him. Rich, protected, selfish—"

"He's my father."

"So? You were happy to let him suffer while he thought Izla controlled me."

"I thought life would be easier for both of us if Da tried to be humble for a week or two."

"I couldn't have pretended to be what I'm not."

"Because of your pride?"

"Because I'd have to give a demonstration of my power. For Talivane, if not for Mondivinaw. Not having any would make that a little difficult."

"Maybe so. You still didn't have to throw a snit."

"A snit?" I stared at her. "Sometimes I don't think you're human."

"I'm not. I'm a witch."

"You should be human first, no matter what common folk say."

"Spare me your patronizing tone, hmm?"

We stared at each other for a long moment. "If you spare me," I said at last, beginning to smile.

She frowned, then nodded. "You're right. I'm sorry, Rifkin."

"I'm sorry too. What do you want to do about your father?"

"Let him worry. It'll be good for him."

"Do you have Harvest Fest in this region?"

"Yes. Why?"

"I want to nominate you for the Queen of Kindness."

She laughed again. "All right, Rifkin. I'll go tell Da to stop sweating."

"Thank you."

"But I'll remind him that Izla could escape."

"Fine." I watched her descend, then rushed after her.

"Forget something?" she asked.

"Yes. My way back."

She sighed. "And this is the defender I found in the woods." She squeezed my hand, so I held hers, and we returned the way we had come. Talivane stood outside Mondivinaw's room, and Naiji dropped my hand when she saw him. "Brother!"

He turned. "Where've you been? They said you and Rifkin . . ." He studied me with a sneer.

"We were checking one of the abandoned wings," Naiji said. "It seems secure."

"I should imagine it would be." He continued to look at me. "My father thinks you're a great witch, Rifkin."

"I'm not."

"Chifeo said you were one too."

"He was wrong."

Talivane nodded. "Odd how these rumors spread so quickly."

"Rifkin's as loyal as I am," Naiji said.

"Of course," Talivane answered. "He's bound to you. But how loyal are you, dear sister?"

Naiji's brow furrowed in anger or confusion. "What do you mean?"

"What I said. I thought you believed in our cause, yet you hesitate—"

"I need time, Talivane."

"Time that you spend with that . . ." He pointed at me.

"Careful," I said. "I might bite."

"That . . ." His finger continued to waggle, so I snapped at it. He snatched it back and said, "That little dark monkey of a boundman!"

"Talivane?" I said.

"Yes?"

"Bite my banana."

The whites of his eyes were huge around his grey-green pupils. "Rifkin, you—"

Naiji snatched at his arm. "We need him, dearest. Truly. There are more reasons than you know."

"Oh?" Talivane said coldly.

"Father's not entirely wrong."

"I don't like a mystery."

"I'll tell you more later. Trust me."

"Can I?"

She nodded.

"Come with me."

Naiji glanced from Talivane to me. I said, "I've things to do."

"I'll see you later, then," she said.

Talivane shook his hand as though brushing me away. "Go, monkey."

"What a wit," I said. "How could I ever equal it? Perhaps if I hit my head repeatedly with a rock for half a day? Or if you locked me in a room with only Avarineo for company for ten years—"

"Go," Talivane said. "You have an archery class to teach."

"Oops." I waited a moment, mostly because he wanted me to leave. "Any news of Komaki?"

"His troops are moving," Talivane said. "They'll probably be here by mid-afternoon."

"And what's his wealth?"

"Why?"

"I've been wondering if he might send more Spirits."

Talivane shook his head. "He wouldn't bother to bring his army, then. And I doubt he intends to impoverish himself in this war."

"Good." I left for the courtyard.

Feschian had already set up three bales of hay by the gate and draped each with a sheet that bore the outline of a helmeted warrior. Most of the castle's inhabitants who did not regularly serve on the guard were lined up to take shots at the target. There were perhaps fifteen people in all. Kivakali was among them. They took turns shooting, three at a time with five arrows each.

Feschian nodded to me. "Afternoon, Rifkin."

"It's morning, still."

"Why, so it is. You're up early."

"I've been up for almost two hours."

"Got lost again?"

"I was busy. I forgot about this."

She nodded. "We'll stop soon. I don't want to tire them out."

"Wise." I nodded at the shape-changer, who had put two arrows into the left target. "He's not bad."

"Fat Cat? He's supposed to be shooting at the middle one."

"Oh. What about the rocksmith?"

"I told her to shoot at the left figure. If she didn't decide to try another, she's doing well."

The next group began. The fencer placed five shots in as many seconds into the center of his target. "I'm glad he's on our side," I said.

"Yes. Iron Eyes isn't bad."

"An odd nickname."

"His strength lies in hexing. Other witches, as well as commoners."

"Iron . . . I see." Kivakali took the fencer's bow from him to send an arrow into the wooden gate. "Excuse me," I told Feschian and went to Kivakali. "Lady," I said.

She blushed. "Rifkin, I'm so—"

"You shoot well," I said. "It's merely a matter of concentration." I reached for her bow. "May I?"

"Certainly."

"You worry too much about the mechanics of shooting. Think only of the target." My arrow buried itself in the circle that marked the painted warrior's heart. I gave the bow back to her. "That isn't to say you can ignore the details. If you'll permit me . . ." I stepped behind her to show her as I would a child, so both our hands gripped the bow and the string. "Full extension. Let the far end rest lightly on the fingers holding the bow. The other hand holds the string, not the arrow. Think of the arrow as a bird, and clumsy human hands will injure it. Think of the target as someone you hate. The arrow is a messenger. Its message is death. Understand?"

"Yes."

I let go of her bow, so Kivakali was no longer in my embrace. "Good. Send it. Now!"

She hit the target. Her arrow was outside the warrior's outline, but it was in the target. "Better," I said. "Again."

Two of her next three shots were killing ones. I wondered who she pictured as she aimed.

She smiled at me. "Thank you."

"It's my job, Lady."

"From what you said last night, I wouldn't expect . . ."

"Yes?"

"Well, you suggested I think of killing."

"I thought it would help your shooting. It did."

"That's all?"

"It's what you'll be doing, if your father attacks."

"I know. But—"

"Later, Lady. This is no time for philosophy." I bowed to her and returned to Feschian.

"Well done, Rifkin."

"Thanks."

"You have a way with the women of this castle."

I glanced at her, but Feschian only smiled and watched the next archers.

After half an hour I had them stop for a few simple exercises, then took them all through a long period of meditation.

"What next?" I asked Feschian.

She shrugged. "We're as ready as we'll ever be."

I dismissed the class, telling them to go rest, if they could. I went to find Dovriex. He was in the kitchens, honing his knives. "Something I said?" I asked. He flipped the one he held, and it quivered in the door beside my head. I reached out to withdraw it. "Whatever it was, I apologize."

Dovriex smiled. "Don't bother. I just wanted to see if you'd blink."

"If you'd asked, I would've blinked for half an hour." I flipped the knife back into a cutting block near him. "You blinked too."

"Something in my eye. If you came for a snack, you're out of luck."

"No." I sat cross-legged on a counter. "I came to ask about Kivakali."

"Talivane doesn't like her, but he won't let anyone else have her."

I thought I heard regret behind his joking tone. "Not that. What do you think of her?"

"I think she does well in a difficult situation."

Subtlety was never my strength. "Do you think she'd try to kill Talivane?"

He glanced up. "Why do you care? I thought your bond—" He seemed more curious than annoyed.

"If she tries to kill Naiji as well, I'm concerned."

"That's crazy."

"Someday I'm going to tell someone something, and he'll say 'Rifkin, that's brilliant!' The shock will probably stop my heart."

"Hmm." Dovriex plucked the knife from the chopping block and returned it to its sheath with a spin that, had I tried it, would have opened every vein in my wrist.

I said, "Only the insecure need to show off."

"True. But when I think of the unkind things you've said about my meals—"

"Every one was an understatement."

"Maybe." Dovriex smiled, then frowned. "I might understand why Kivakali would kill Talivane. Why Naiji as well?"

A number of wooden mugs were drying on the counter. I picked up three to juggle as I talked. "If only Talivane died, everyone would suspect Kivakali had a part in it."

"Hmm." Dovriex stepped back to a basket of eggs. In seconds he had four circling through the air in front of him. "It's true that if both Gromandiels were killed by the Spirits, no one would suspect Kivakali. But by that argument, why should she stop with Naiji?"

I snatched up another mug and worked it into my juggling. "For economy's sake," I said.

"Makes some sense," Dovriex said. He added a fifth egg to his pattern. "But the other could just as well be Mondivinaw, then."

"Maybe." The mugs now went behind my back on every second toss. "Except that an enemy of the witches wouldn't worry much about an old man."

"Their mistake." Dovriex added two more eggs, and I decided not to watch him anymore.

"Perhaps. Perhaps they'll try to kill Mondivinaw also," I said. Doubting it was wise, I got a candlestick going with the mugs. The balance was tricky. "Still, Naiji'd be the logical choice to divert suspicion."

"Granted," Dovriex said, then added in a softer tone, "Nine."

"Show-off," I said. "So what do you think?"

"I think you'll drop them in thirty seconds, at most."

"About Kivakali."

"Oh. I like her. I'd rather—" He began to laugh as the mugs fell. The candlestick was definitely a mistake.

I looked at Dovriex. Nine eggs still circled through the air. Without any encouragement from his hands.

"You bastard," I said.

He laughed. "Some people can't take a joke."

"You lousy witch bastard."

"Want to see what else I can do with these eggs?"

"Send any this way and I'll eat them."

"Oops." He let them settle back in their basket.

I said, "I thought you couldn't do tricks like that."

"I couldn't, before. I think it's from the strain of knowing that Komaki's coming. Everything seems more..." Dovriex held up his hands like he wanted to grab something. "...more intense. Time moves differently, in spurts rather than a flow. Know what I mean?"

"Too well."

"I started to drop one of those eggs earlier, and it just stopped in midair when I wanted it to. I've been studying levitation for years, and today..." Dovriex shook his head. "It worked. Just like that."

"Great," I said. "You can throw eggs at Komaki's men. Hey! Your knives..."

Dovriex nodded. "They're steel. This must be another exception to the laws of iron, but I don't know what the trick is. I've been near steel, cooking things for years, and all of a sudden, I can do a tiny bit of magic."

Interesting, Izla whispered. I bit my lip, then said, "How long until lunch?"

"Who said there was lunch?"

"Oh. Will there be dinner?"

"Yes." He smiled cruelly. "Warmed—"

"Don't tell me, man! Let me dream a little, eh?"

"Sure. It'll be better than—"

I ran from the kitchen with my ears covered. One of the twins walked by, peering at me from the corners of her eyes. "Ah, hello, Sivifal," I said.

"Livifal."

"Of course. Sorry." Feschian was right. I was making quite an impression on the women of this castle.

One task remained. I found the armory, where a glum fellow stood guard. "I'm here to look at the musket," I told him.

"A student of rust, eh?" He pointed. "So, look."

It was not a musket. It was a piece of pipe with a broken wooden stock that had been left on the ground for at least a year before it was brought there. A smith might make a gun of it again, but I suspected the smith would begin by melting it down and reforging it.

"Thanks," I told the guard.

"S'all right. I was tired of armory duty. It's nice to be on the museum shift for a while."

I went to my room and bathed, then dressed again, to nap in my clothes with my weapons at my side. I woke thinking my head was in a kettle and someone was beating on the outside, then realized that the great bronze bell I had noticed in one tower still worked. Someone was ringing the alarm. Komaki was here.

16

CASTLE
GROMANDIEL

I SNATCHED UP my helmet and axe and swordbelt and ran. "Lady Naiji!" I shouted. She did not answer, so I assumed she was already on the walls. I dashed along the halls and down the stairs and into the courtyard. It was empty. I looked up. The sun had finished three-fourths of her daily trek through the skies. The alarm bell no longer rang. I wondered for an instant if I had dreamt the warning, then looked to my left. Almost all the inhabitants of Castle Gromandiel stood on the parapet by the southwestern wall.

I turned around, thinking this was not how Feschian had planned it. I saw a soldier or two on each of the other walls, and three by the front gate. Someone had probably decided to put as many people as possible where Komaki would see them, to give him a false idea of our strength. I wondered if they expected the Duke to think the helmeted children were dwarfs.

I climbed to join the others. Several nodded to me. Naiji and Talivane stood together, so I walked over to Feschian.

"Morning," she said to me.

"I was taking a nap."

"Some of us need all the beauty sleep we can get."

I looked out. Tents were rising in a field perhaps a quarter of a mile away. "How many do you think?" I asked.

"Enough."

I glanced at her.

"Over a hundred. Less than two hundred. The Duke may have convinced one of the lords to be his ally, but not the Queen. Not yet, anyway."

"Will they attack today?"

Feschian looked at the sky. Perhaps four hours of daylight remained. "I would."

"And we're ready?"

"You could call it that."

"Will they send someone to offer terms?"

"Probably. Not that it'll matter."

"Why?"

"You'll see."

I looked to learn if anyone was missing. Avarineo was absent, but both Livifal and Sivifal were there. The giant was probably at his post by the cliff wall. Fat Cat the shape-changer and Iron Eyes the fencer stood with their arms about each other's shoulders, as if they might be more than friends. Dovriex was with Naiji and Talivane. I thought he looked odd with a bow rather than kitchen tools in his hands. He still wore his multiple sheath of knives on one hip.

Most of the others were still faces without names to me. I recognized the woman they called the rocksmith, who was hugging the little girl that I thought might be a Master Artist in a few years with perseverance and the right teacher. There was a small boy who always stared at me, making me wonder if I'd spilled something on my pants. There was an older boy of Chifeo's age who had an odd twitch, and the girl who had flirted with me during my first class. There were some twenty people in all, counting children and babies, and perhaps six or seven at other posts. I wondered how many would still be alive tomorrow morning.

"Where's Kivakali?" I asked.

"In the main keep. Talivane's orders."

I left Feschian. Passing by Iron Eyes and Fat Cat, I heard Iron Eyes say "Be careful, Fat Cat."

Fat Cat said peevishly, "I wish I could lose that name."

Iron Eyes smiled. "Lose some weight."

"Sometimes I wish you'd lose your tongue."

"No you don't. Then I couldn't—"

Feeling like an eavesdropper, I walked faster. Private conversations were going on all around me, though. I could not escape them.

The little blond girl was telling the rocksmith, "But, Mama, I don't want to stay in the tower with the babies! I want to stay here with you!"

The rocksmith shook her head. "You won't be staying with the babies, Tikiji. You'll be there with Sivifal, helping her protect the little ones. Okay? You'll do this for me?"

"But—"

"Please?"

Tikiji nodded solemnly. "For you, Mama."

They hugged again, and I walked faster yet.

Naiji and Dovriex both smiled at me, and Talivane sneered. When I said "Surrender," the smiles disappeared.

"No," Talivane said, looking out over the field. Two riders were leaving Komaki's camp and riding toward the road to our front gate.

"I've been thinking about this," I said.

Talivane said, "Don't strain yourself."

"Komaki's reason for coming here is that these lands were a part of his duchy."

"More than a thousand years ago," Talivane said. "What he really wants is the Queen and—"

"Don't go into that," I said. "His stated reason is that these lands were once a part of his."

"Yes," Talivane said.

"Then swear allegiance to him," I said. "You'll win time, if nothing else."

"You think so?'

"Yes," I said.

"You're a stranger here."

"Thanks for telling me. So?"

Talivane turned away to watch the two riders approach.

"So?" I repeated.

Naiji said, "There were witches who lived on Komaki's lands, Rifkin. A few months ago he had them all brought to his castle, tied to stakes, and burnt. That'll happen to us, if we acknowledge him as our lord."

Dovriex clapped me on the shoulder. "We're not dead yet, Rifkin."

"True." I kept from adding, "So?"

The riders came to the little road that wound up the mountainside. Most of us strode to the gate wall to watch. As they came closer, I saw they were two young women. Red plumes affixed to their helmets proclaimed them officers. The drawbridge had been raised hours ago, so they reined up before it. One called, "Greetings to the lord of Gromandiel!"

"Grim greetings, it would seem," Talivane said.

"Make of them what you will, Count Gromandiel." The one who spoke was larger and older than the other. Both wore coats of mail, but only the speaker carried a musket across her saddle. "Do you refuse to entertain your master and his followers?"

"I never said I would not entertain Komaki," Talivane said. "But I will not allow him in my castle."

"You refuse him his rights as your master?"

Talivane sighed. "He is not my master. He never has been my master, nor will he ever be my master."

"You admit—"

"I tire of this," Talivane said. "Komaki's game of legal truths has always been an ugly farce. I will not play it."

The older woman drew herself up on her horse. "In that case, rebel, I have no choice but to declare—"

"Leave," Talivane said. "And if you're fools, come back with your master's warriors. Out of respect for the Queen's Law, I give you this one chance."

The woman pointed at Talivane. "You're the one who makes a mockery of all we value."

Talivane snapped both hands before him as though he flicked water from them, and they blazed with light. "You have been warned," he said. "Say another word, and you die."

"So say you, witch bastard!" The woman swung her musket to her shoulder.

Lightning flared from Talivane's hands. The woman and

her horse both convulsed and fell. The other officer fought to
control her mount, then wheeled it and fled. Talivane called
after her, "Tell Komaki that we are not helpless! Tell him he
cannot hide, not behind iron or mercenaries! Tell him to leave
us or he dies!"

Naiji looked at the dead officer and horse. "What of—"

"Ignore it," her brother said. "There'll be more there, soon."
He glanced at me. "You look ill, bold warrior."

"I am."

"What should I have done?"

I did not know, so I looked away.

Talivane said, "In battle, stay far from me. I doubt it would
be safe for either of us if I use lightning and you're too close
with your steel."

I said nothing. Perhaps Dovriex's egg-juggling proved that
a witch could become accustomed to iron, but it also suggested
that the process was a slow one. For every witch who had
carefully avoided iron, the old rules still held. I would stay
away from Talivane.

Naiji said, "Do you think we have a chance of surviving,
now?"

I shrugged. "How many times can he do that, before he's
too exhausted to continue?"

She swallowed. "Maybe . . . maybe ten times."

I touched her arm and smiled. "If it's the right ten times,
it'll help."

Talivane turned to face his people. He raised his arms and
said, "This is your last chance! If any of you would risk Komaki's hospitality, go now! We will not dare open our gates
again until he leaves our valley!"

No one spoke until Iron Eyes said, "No, Lord. We're with
you."

"Thank you. To your posts, then."

More than half the group left for their positions on the walls.
There were four of us who had no assigned locations: Talivane,
Naiji, Feschian, and me. A fifth if you counted Mondivinaw,
but the infirmary was his post. Or so I thought until I saw him
hobbling across the courtyard with his crutch.

"Da!" Naiji cried.

"Father! Get back to bed, you damned—" Talivane was

silent for a second, undoubtedly listening to Mondivinaw's mindspeech. "I'm sorry, but—" And he was silent again. "As you will, Father." He pointed at two guards. "Carry him up here. Then fetch his chair. He has as much right to be here as any of us." Talivane winced, then added, "More."

The Count tried to have Mondivinaw's chair placed by the cliff wall. The old man refused. His chair was finally placed directly over the main gate, where the attack would be worst.

Naiji glanced his way, then said, "He asks if the great lord still thinks him a coward."

"No. I think him a fool."

She nodded, then smiled, then said, "He says the great lord is probably right, but he would rather die here than in a sick-room."

Komaki's warriors marched out from their tents. They sang something that was punctuated with triumphal cries. If it was intended to make us uneasy, it worked.

Someone near me was singing along, quietly and sadly. I glanced to see Feschian. She nodded her chin in time to the words, and a few tears streaked her cheeks.

I nudged Naiji. "What?"

"She served Komaki as his captain," Naiji whispered. "They might have been more than that."

"Even though she was a witch?"

"She didn't know until fairly recently. A lot of us are that way."

"I see."

Feschian looked up and grinned coldly. "It's a war song, Rifkin. In this land mercenaries call themselves part of the Confederacy of Steel. I was one of them, once."

She turned away from us. I said, "You're welcome to use my axe, if you'd like."

She shook her head. "No. Thanks just the same."

Naiji said, "Rifkin, if you're keeping your iron . . ."

I nodded. "I know. Stay away from the rest of you."

"At least five feet. And don't get in the path of a spell."

"I won't."

Feschian jerked her thumb at Komaki's army. "Five gold pieces say they attack the southwest wall first."

I shook my head. "The gate. It's easier terrain and—"

"Talk with your gold or not at all."

Naiji said, "How can you sit there making bets while they're coming?"

"It's expected of warriors," I said. "We prefer bets and jokes to soiling our pants."

Feschian nodded. "We do that later."

"You should probably go inside soon," I told Naiji.

"Hardly," she said.

"Why?"

Naiji jerked her chin to indicate Talivane and Feschian, who waited on the wall.

"Don't be brave," I said.

"I'm not. I'm terrified."

"Then go."

"I'm more afraid of being a coward."

"You're making this difficult."

She smiled thinly. "You're the one who decided that being bound to me meant being my personal guard."

"Doesn't matter. I'd prefer you were inside, where it's safer."

"I win," Feschian said.

Naiji and I both glanced at her. Feschian said, "It's the southwest wall."

I jumped to my feet and stared. "They're fools."

"Not so. We'll be stretched too thinly to defend it properly. And then if they send a smaller party at the gate—"

"Go into the main keep, Naiji," I said. "Now."

"No, Rifkin. You're bound, remember?"

"Many of these people will need healing, Naiji. You can't help them if you're dead."

"I could help one, Rifkin. Maybe two, if I exhausted myself. Then I'd be useless for anything else. There are those who know more about common forms of medicine than I, and they're in the keep. I'm staying here."

"I . . ." Reluctantly, I nodded. "You shouldn't make it so easy for me to be free again," I said, touching her wrist.

"Poor Rifkin."

Feschian said softly, "Damn."

"What?"

"I thought those were supply carts. They're cannons."

I stared where she pointed. A detachment of riders had separated from the main body of foot soldiers. They accompanied two ox-drawn cannons on the castle road.

"What can we do?" I asked.

"We can give them a surprise," Feschian said. "Rocksmith!"

The plump woman hurried over, trotting more than running, though she puffed with exertion. She seemed better suited to bake cookies for children than to cope with cannons.

Feschian pointed at the riders.

"Now?" the rocksmith asked.

"Yes."

The rocksmith nodded and sat cross-legged on the parapet. Her eyes closed and she rested her palms against the stone under her.

Naiji smiled, satisfied. She was not looking at Komaki's riders, but at the mountain stream that had made the castle moat its bed. I glanced from Naiji to the stream to the rocksmith to Feschian, then scratched my head and waited.

Six of us were above the gate, counting Mondivinaw and a boy who probably should have been put with the children. The approaching riders might have numbered thirty, perhaps a few more. I looked back to the valley. Komaki's warriors already began the long climb up the southwest slope. I fastened the chin strap of my iron and leather helmet, then began to whistle the opening measures of the death song.

Naiji glanced at me. "That's pretty."

"Out of context, perhaps." I looked down at the moat. No water flowed through it. My gaze flicked to the stream. Somehow, the rocksmith had diverted it from its usual course. It poured onto the road and raced toward the riders and the cannon carts.

The attackers tried to turn, of course, and they failed, of course. I wished the stream were larger, enough to wash them away. Still, it changed the road into a bed of ice water, rocks, and mud. The oxen would eventually pull their cargo near enough to threaten us, but that would be a matter of hours now, not minutes.

"The riders are coming on," I said.

Mondivinaw stood up from his chair and dragged himself to one of the crenellations to watch. I wanted to say something, but that might force him to answer me with mindspeech, and that might make Izla react.

Naiji picked up a bow. I tucked my axe into my belt to do

the same. Feschian said, "Not yet. We don't want to waste any arrows."

The riders were ninety yards away and slowed by the stream. The afternoon sun glinted on their helmets. Their dark cloaks flapped behind them like batwings. Almost all carried bows, but a few had muskets. I wondered if they could shoot from the saddle, as the plainsfolk were said to do. When the riders were sixty yards from us, I glanced at Feschian. She nodded.

My shot took someone, young or old, male or female, loved or unloved, in the chest. I whistled the next measure of the death song and released a second arrow.

A few musket shots came from the southwest, but there was no time to look to see what happened there. Unless our people stood on top of the walls to be targets, they were safe enough from guns. I was saving my worries for when the enemy was close enough to shower us with arrows.

Feschian and Naiji were each ten or fifteen feet from me. They fired as quickly as they could. The boy cringed against the wall. In each hand was a quiver of arrows, ready to bring to us when we needed them. Mondivinaw stood at his post, twitching his good hand with a perverse glee. I couldn't take time to see what effect his spells had, but it seemed that not every rider who fell had been hit with an arrow.

A musketeer leaped to the ground to aim up at us. Feschian's arrow might have taken her before mine did. Another tried to fire from the saddle. The recoil knocked him to the ground, and I pinned him through the stomach before he could stand.

Most of their cavalry used their bows from horseback. Most of their arrows shattered against the castle walls. We had the advantage here and they knew it. Shrieking and waving, they turned back. We had repulsed the first charge.

Seven cloaked warriors lay in the muddy stream. I suspected as many others were too badly wounded to continue. I decided to be realistic and assume there had been two hundred of them. "Only one hundred and eighty-six to go," I told Feschian.

"My," she said. "I do feel much better knowing that."

I wanted to stay there and rest, but the fight continued at the southwest wall. The sky seemed to rain arrows. I saw the top of a scaling ladder appear, but the boy with the twitch scrambled up to push it away. When an arrow caught him, he fell from the wall with the enemy's ladder.

I snatched a wooden shield from a pile of ancient weapons, our one surplus in this affair, to cover myself as I ran to the other wall. I shouted at Naiji to stay behind, but she didn't, of course.

Another scaling ladder poked up far from me. The rocksmith saw it and put her hands against the castle wall. A moment later a helmeted head appeared at the top of the ladder, then disappeared with a scream as his ladder slid sideways. The rocksmith nodded to herself.

I picked a crenellation for my own and pretended for the next few minutes that this was only a carnival game. Step back against the wall, snatch an arrow from the quiver at my feet, fit it to the string. Step into the open, pick a target, fire. Step back behind the wall, snatch up the next arrow. It was a simple game, yet I found it harder each time to step out and shoot.

The pretense of a game ended when I stepped out and a bearded face peered at me, only a few feet away. We stared long enough for me to notice the flecks of grey in his eyebrows, the missing upper teeth in his open mouth. His eyes went wide, and his mouth opened even more, perhaps to plead with me. I wonder now what he could have said. He might have been there because soldiering was his only means of earning money to feed his family, or maybe he had been forced to join the army by Komaki's warriors. And maybe he was one of those who think killing is a fine and noble occupation. I released my arrow. It took him through his open mouth, and he fell.

The tip of his ladder was barely visible. I poked it away with my bow, then resumed the game of shooting. When a horn sounded in the distance, the attackers retreated, firing at us as they backed away.

The pretty girl of Chifeo's age was still shooting. "Stop," I said. "They're too far."

She continued, desperately fitting arrows to her bow and straining to fire. Her fingers were bloody, cut by the string. I grabbed her shoulder. She suddenly collapsed against me, crying, "They got Ifkanian! They got Ifkanian!"

"I'm sorry," I said, wondering if Ifkanian was the boy with the tic. I put my arm around the girl and felt entirely useless.

Feschian walked by, glancing our way without speaking. She wore a stained bandage on her left arm. She halted and nodded to me, then reached out to take the girl away, still saying nothing. I watched them go.

Komaki's forces were regrouping on the plain below. Naiji touched my elbow and said, "It's not over? For today, even?"

I shook my head. "This attack was only to test our strength. And to see if they could scare us. The next one will decide whether we're in for a short war or a long one."

≋ 17 ≋

CASTLE
GROMANDIEL

I COUNTED BODIES, since that was an easy thing to do. There might have been fifteen on the southwest slope. That was worse than Komaki planned, I was sure. He never expected us to hinder his cannons. If he had succeeded in blasting open the gates for his cavalry while the foot soldiers stormed our walls, his war would already have ended.

Naiji had gone inside to help the healers. I would have preferred to sit in some secluded place with her, saying nothing, perhaps holding hands, perhaps hugging, perhaps stripping each other's clothes off and . . . I went in search of Talivane. He was kneeling beside a boy of ten or eleven years. The boy's chest was blood-soaked, and his face was pale. Talivane was telling the boy how brave he had been and how the healers would make him better as soon as they could. I might have had some sympathy for Talivane then, if I didn't still believe this was all his fault for refusing to leave Castle Gromandiel. A guard picked up the boy in her arms and carried him away.

"You ready to repeat your lightning tricks?" I asked.

"Why?"

"Two cannons. Komaki's sent men and horses to help haul them up the stream. They'll be in place soon. Feschian may have mentioned them."

"She did."

"Once they're set up, we're finished."

"I know. But I don't know if I can—"

"Try, Gromandiel."

He nodded wearily. "I intend to."

"Better do it soon."

He nodded and beckoned to Feschian, who was directing the care of the wounded and the gathering of arrows. When Feschian came, Talivane said, "I'll attempt the cannons."

Feschian nodded. "I've been trying to think of another way, but—"

"Just do it," I said.

Talivane smiled. "You are impetuous, little southerner."

"What's the delay?"

"We must have a stretcher brought up here."

I looked around. Several people had been wounded so badly that they were being taken into the main keep, and I'd seen them carry away a middle-aged woman whose skull had been crushed by a musket ball. Everyone who remained was capable of standing or leaning against the wall.

"Why?" I said.

Talivane flicked his hand toward the cannons. "Because I must do something greater than I've ever done before. I'd prefer to be kept in relative comfort, if I lose consciousness."

I grunted noncommittally and left him. At least two of his people would never know any more comfort at all.

I went to the wall and leaned against it, watching. The road was steep and had never been well maintained. Now that it was a streambed, it was almost impassable for carts. Komaki's soldiers bunched behind the cannons to push and tied ropes to the front to pull. They sang their damned war song as they worked. I sat there thinking, *I am going to die. And then I won't ache so much.*

The destruction of the cannons was a simple thing. While the stretcher-bearers stood near, Talivane took a position at the center of the parapet, directly over the gates. He raised both hands above his head, seeming to pray or possibly to rest while he focused his thoughts on his power, and then shouted something in a language I did not understand while he lowered his hands to aim them at the cannons. The lightning gushed from his fingertips like fireworks.

The warriors by the carts screamed and died. So did the oxen. So did several soldiers who were only standing in the water too close to the carts. Then one cart exploded, and then the other, and then Komaki's followers—the ones who still lived—ran, screaming in fear, back toward their camps.

Most of the witches began to cheer. I turned and threw up. I straightened up after a moment, expecting Talivane's sneer. Instead I saw that he had spoken the truth to me about this experiment. He lay as though dead on a stretcher borne by two guards, and they carried him away to the main keep. His hands were charred and bleeding.

Feschian noticed me and said, "You okay?"

"Sure," I said. "I just wondered if breakfast would taste better the second time around." I nodded at the bandage on her arm. "How's that?"

"I've had worse."

"We could write a pamphlet," I said, "on how to talk like soldiers and fools."

"Fine," Feschian said. "I'll write the part about soldiers."

Komaki's officers were having trouble forcing their fighters to regroup. They had believed that witches were helpless before iron. Now they might think us invulnerable, if we could frighten them again. "How long before Talivane regains his strength?"

Feschian shrugged. "At least a day, I'd imagine."

The singing began anew. A few of the cavalry rode toward us as though daring us to do anything. They stayed just out of arrowshot and shouted their speculations about our parentage and personal habits. I took a bow and proved that one fellow wasn't quite beyond our range, which quieted them for a while.

Feschian ordered most of our fighters from the southwest wall to take positions over the gate. Komaki's forces began to trot toward us. I asked, "What's the supply of arrows?"

"Almost half gone."

"I would've felt better if you'd said that half remained."

Dovriex had taken a position on Feschian's far side. He called, "Rifkin!"

"Yes?"

"Half of this morning's porridge remains for future meals."

"Nobody likes a wiseass chef."

Feschian fired the first arrow, and the rest of us joined her. I wondered which of the plumed riders was Komaki, or if any of them were. I was glad that Naiji was safe in the castle, then remembered that Kivakali was there too. Well, better that Naiji should be with one suspected killer than facing two hundred confirmed ones.

This attack was more orderly. Before, each warrior had run alone, crouched behind a shield until finding a protected place from which to shoot at us. Now they advanced in rows. The soldiers in front locked shields, and the ones in back fired. Then the front row opened to let the back row pass, and the process repeated itself. I wondered how long Komaki's officers had drilled his people. The mad rush of the first assault was obviously the Konds' preferred practice.

When they were close, a party of axemen rushed for the gates. Arrows had no effect on the ceiling they made of their shields, but Avarineo began to hurl rocks that were bigger than watermelons. Three axemen fell. The rest, seven or eight, made it to the gates. I turned to Feschian and saw that she had anticipated this. Several children were bringing kettles of hot oil from the kitchens.

I concentrated on my archery, trying to pick musketeers and officers for targets. When the axemen began to scream below us, I whistled the death song louder. When my mouth grew too dry to whistle, I hummed it. Killing is easy if you refrain from thinking, *Ah! There goes someone's father. Ah! And there a lover. Ah! A sister, undoubtedly, and probably a cousin as well*.

A shout came from the southwest wall. Several of Komaki's men had reached the parapet. The rocksmith put her hands on the wall to repeat her earlier trick of toppling the ladder. I saw the ladder go, but that did nothing about the four soldiers who had climbed over. One brought his sword in an arc that half severed the rocksmith's neck.

Several of us turned to run to the other wall. Feschian, her face grim, said, "Rifkin and Dovriex! The rest stay here, damn your eyes!"

Dovriex's arrow took the man who had killed the rocksmith. Mine skidded on a woman's chain mail and lodged in her shoulder. The three intruders, including the one I had wounded, raced for the stairs, certainly to try to open our gates from within.

I dropped my bow, pulled my axe from my belt, and leaped down. There was a stair landing fifteen feet below me, and I hit harder than I would have liked. Another ladder had appeared at the southwest wall. "Dovriex! Help the others! I'll take these!" Telling this now, it sounds like bravado. The truth is that it was necessity or stupidity. I take it as a compliment that Dovriex did not question me. He fired another arrow that broke on one intruder's mail, then turned to go to the other wall.

I jumped from the landing, another fifteen feet or so, and had to steady myself with my right hand. As soon as I touched, I stood, snatched a throwing dart from my belt, and whipped it into the face of the woman closest to me. It caught her in one eye, and she stumbled.

The remaining two moved to pass me on either side, thinking that I would pick one while the other reached the gate. I chose the unwounded one, a boy with a young face. Our encounter was nothing a poet would want to write about, not a duel that occurred between two warriors who found privacy in the midst of battle. I feinted with the axe, then took the boy with a thrust of the short sword to his throat.

The wounded woman was almost to the gate. Had I been kinder, I might have let her touch it. I threw the axe at the back of her helmet, and she fell forward. Then, because I had no rope or time to tie any of them, I stabbed each of the three in the back to be sure they were dead.

More intruders were on the southwest wall, yet the assault on the front gate continued. I noticed that Iron Eyes kept several warriors away from Fat Cat, who stripped himself of armor and clothing. I had seen greater acts of insanity on battlefields before, so I did not watch longer. Dovriex was using a pike like a staff to keep several of the Konds from approaching our bowmen by the gate. The rest of our guards on the southwest wall were busy in a desperate game of pushing away ladders.

The next part of the battle is still a blur to me. I went to Dovriex's aid, and then, for long minutes, we fought back Komaki's forces. A plump panther helped to create chaos, initially for our side as much as for the other. Feschian sent Avarineo and a few more fighters to join us, and we battled with no more strategy than tavern brawlers, though the results were far deadlier. At last, when witches were the only ones left alive on the walls of Castle Gromandiel, eight of our people lay dead and three more were seriously wounded.

Feschian, watching the retreat, said, "If they'd continued the attack for five minutes more—"

"Don't undervalue us," I said. "Six." I let my axe fall to the ground and slumped down to sit. The sun was close to setting. The air was cold. Iron Eyes was dead, and Fat Cat, naked and human, cradled the fencer's head in his lap as he cried. Livifal or Sivifal was badly wounded. She might not live out the night. The girl who had lamented the loss of the boy with the twitch now had an arm to add to her losses. I saw Dovriex by the rocksmith's body and remembered the woman's daughter who waited in the main keep.

Feschian said, "What are you singing?"

"The death song."

"Who for?"

"All of us."

18

CASTLE
GROMANDIEL

"WILL THEY ATTACK after dark?" I asked Feschian.

"There's a saying, never fright a witch at night. I doubt they'll dare visit us this evening. We'll still have guards out, of course."

I nodded. "You never know when they might change an old saying."

I helped Dovriex carry his sister into the castle. The dining hall had become the new infirmary, since it was on the ground floor and the nearby kitchens could provide food and fresh water. Kivakali bustled about as though the witches were her own people, speaking a few words of comfort to one and bringing a bedpan to another.

One of the red-haired twins came over to us. When she saw who we bore, she gasped, covering her mouth with her hand. I felt as if this would all be easier if I knew which one we carried and which stood before us. Dovriex said, "Sivifal, I'm..." His words trailed off. I discovered that knowledge only made me feel worse.

Sivifal pointed at a number of mattresses that had been dragged into the room. Most were occupied by the wounded, and a few by the dead. "Put her there." Her tone mixed urgency and efficiency, saying clearly that she would treat her sister like all her other patients.

Naiji sat with her hands on the brow of the girl who had lost an arm. Both had their eyes closed, but then Naiji opened hers. "Rifkin."

I gestured at the girl. "Is she—"

Naiji closed her eyes again, then said "No." She looked at me and shook her head. "You need bandaging."

"Later," I said.

"Now."

"Yes, Lady."

We moved away from the dead girl. I took off my coat and let Naiji wash my chest. I tried not to wince.

"Were there as many scars on this body when you first occupied it?"

"None."

"You should treat borrowed things better than you do."

"Perhaps."

"Da's dead."

I turned to stare at her. She nodded.

"I hadn't heard."

"I haven't either."

"But how—"

"He and I, we . . ." Her voice was close to breaking, so I took her hand in mine and held it.

"We shared similar gifts, Rifkin. He was the stronger mind-speaker, but my skills at sensing were . . ." She paused often, almost after every word. Each time, I thought she would cry, but she did not. "My skills were like his. Once I fell down in the woods, and Da came to find me. I never thought it meant anything more than, well, fathers do that."

I nodded.

"And once he was away for weeks. I woke in the middle of a night, convinced that something terrible had happened to him. When he came back, he said robbers had beaten him and left him for dead. But I never thought we were linked until . . ." She held me with her gaze. "Until I felt him go."

"I'm sorry."

"You hated him."

"I didn't know him."

"No," she said. "You didn't."

We remained there for a moment, holding hands. Someone moaned, and Naiji went to help.

I found Dovriex in the kitchens, tending something in a kettle. "Smells like venison," I said.

"It is. Stew."

"That'll be nice."

"If there was more time, I'd fix something better."

"Stew'll be nice."

"I was saving some mushrooms."

"I like mushrooms," I said.

"I'll use a lot, then."

"Your sister is . . ."

He glanced at me.

"She's still alive, Dovriex. That's not much, but it's something."

"She never liked mushrooms."

"Don't use them if—"

"I'll use them. This dinner will be my masterpiece, Rifkin."

"I'm sure it will."

"If I had more time, I'd bake something."

"That's all right. Everyone likes stew. Especially venison stew."

"Rum and raisin pudding for dessert," Dovriex said. "Livifal loved my rum and raisin pudding."

I left the kitchens wishing he would just fix the damned porridge again.

The dead were being taken to the cellar. Feschian carried Mondivinaw by herself. We put each body on a blanket on the cool stone floor and left them there. I wondered if Komaki's soldiers would bury us if they won, or burn us. I did not know what northerners did with their dead, but I saw that they cared, and cried as freely as any Ladizhan. Fat Cat mourned there, with the rocksmith's daughter and several others. I fled that room as quickly and as discreetly as I could.

Feschian followed me. We walked in silence until I said, "How many left?"

"That can fight?"

I nodded.

"Counting the hearth cat?"

"If it'll fight."

Feschian ticked off names on her fingers. "You. Me. Avarineo. Dovriex. Sivifal. Fat Cat. Kivakali." She caught my glance and said, "You asked how many could fight, not would. Evrian, Thessaval, and Baldriath. They're members of the castle guard, and competent."

"That's all?"

"There are a few others who would die well, but fight badly. And there're the children."

"How many of them?"

"Seven."

"What about Talivane?"

"You saw his hands. When he comes to, he'll be next to useless."

"Naiji couldn't heal him?"

"She uses her magic sparingly. She's saved several from death today, Rifkin."

"Still—"

"She can't pick favorites. Could you?"

"No." Part of me thought that Naiji had done no kindnesses for those she saved. Another part said that she would have done better to help her brother, so he could help those of us who still lived. And another part said it did not matter. Komaki would try once or twice more to storm Castle Gromandiel. If those attempts failed, he would wait while we starved, and laugh whether Talivane sent ten thousand lightning bolts at his soldiers or not.

Dinner was a dismal affair. We ate in the kitchen, since the dining hall was taken by the wounded. At times the quiet would be broken by a groan or a request from the other room. In the middle of dessert Avarineo held up a spoonful of rum and raisin pudding and said, "This is good stuff! Dovriex should fix this stuff every day!"

We all ignored him. Avarineo looked sad, but he still asked for seconds.

I toured the walls alone. Our guard posts were parodies of defense. The watchers were too tired to watch well and too far apart to watch efficiently. When I returned to my room, Naiji was naked in my sheets. I sat on the edge of the pallet and held her while she cried. "We're all going to die," she finally whispered. "Aren't we? Aren't we?"

I undressed slowly, being careful of my bandages. "Turn over," I said.

"Why?"

"Turn over." She obeyed, and I began to massage her shoulders and her arms. Her entire back was tense, so I kneaded it, then pounded it gently with the sides of my hands, then kneaded it more. I worked the pressure points along her spine by pressing when she exhaled, releasing when she breathed in. When I moved to her buttocks, she tensed again, then relaxed. I worked her thighs and her calves.

When I finished with her feet, I turned her slowly. I put my fingertips against her forehead to soothe her temples, then moved down her cheeks and along her jaw. I did each arm and her pectoral muscles. I rubbed her belly as though she were a cat. I worked the front of her thighs and on down to her feet then up along the inside of her legs. I put her feet against my stomach and pushed her legs against her chest, then let them down. And then I began to retrace the route of my hands with my tongue.

We both found our release only minutes later. I let myself collapse on Naiji. Perhaps we slept for a bit after that.

"Rifkin?"

"Mmm?"

"Thank you."

"No. Thank you."

"No. Thank *you*."

"I just said that."

"No, you didn't. You said, thank you. But I said, thank *you*."

"Oh."

And then we may have slept a little longer.

"Rifkin?"

"Mmm?"

"I'm sorry I brought you into this."

"Shh."

"I don't know what to do."

I kissed her. Her cheeks were damp with tears and her lips and tongue tasted of salt. I had thought it would be a short kiss, until I felt her hand on my buttocks.

"Rifkin?" She gasped her question as she ground her hips against me.

"Yes?"

"I like you, Rifkin. I really do like you."

"I like you, Naiji. You might've noticed."

Her laugh ended with a bark of pleasure as I pressed more tightly. "I love—"

I covered her mouth with mine. We struggled in the dark like fighters. I cannot say who won. Perhaps we both lost, though there was a moment when our cries would have frightened anyone who passed in the hall.

"Naiji?"

"Mmm?"

"Come with me."

"I did."

"No. Away."

She shook her head where it rested on my arm. "I won't leave them, Rifkin."

I wondered if *them* meant the witches or only Talivane. Whatever the shortcomings I saw in Count Gromandiel, he inspired loyalty in his followers. Perhaps I should have said something more to Naiji, but I could think of nothing that might convince her, just as I could think of nothing earlier to convince Feschian. They were all bound to him by love or loyalty. I, bound to Naiji, seemed to be the only free person in the entire hold. I only nodded to Naiji and kissed her forehead.

"G'night, Rifkin."

"Good night, Lady," I said, and finding a pressure point, I made sure she would not wake for several hours.

I dressed and hurried into the cold, dark hall. I worried that I would meet Feschian, but I met no one. Thinking of Feschian made me remember the midnight screams. It was too early for them, if Talivane was awake and had fetched Chifeo or the remaining Spirit to his chambers.

I had noticed a rope in the stables, which meant crossing the courtyard. The moon was almost full, though storm clouds marched across his face. Gromandiel's guards would be watching for movement beyond the castle walls, not within. Nonetheless, I crept through shadows by the main keep and crossed to the empty stable while the moon was obscured for a moment.

An owl fluttered away as I entered, making me wonder if it was one of the witchfolk's friends. I found the rope, a serviceable one of thick hemp, on a nail by an abandoned stall.

I threw it over my shoulder and headed for the walls.

I took the stairs as though this was only another inspection by that nosy little southerner. When one guard called "Who's there?" I said "Rifkin," and that comforted her. I walked on until I came to the middle of the southeast wall. Thirty feet below me was the ledge where I had climbed with Naiji to Castle Gromandiel. I immediately looked for Avarineo, but the lower post had been abandoned when we all retreated into the castle and sealed its gates.

I uncoiled most of my rope, found its center, and encircled a jutting block of the wall by bringing either end of the line through two crenellations. Then, holding both halves of the rope, I lowered myself over the castle wall. At the bottom I released one end, pulled on the other, and it fell beside me.

The stable rope was not as long as the line Avarineo had lowered when Naiji and I came up the face of the cliff. I knew the southwest slope would be watched by nervous soldiers of both sides, but I also knew I was too poor a mountaineer to take the southeast face in the dark. I stooped to gather dirt and rocks. I smeared the dirt on my hands and face and clothes, dropped dirt and rocks into my jacket pocket, and headed toward the slope to Komaki's camp.

The Duke kept a ring of campfires around Castle Gromandiel, each within hailing distance of another. If his guards were good, there would be several warriors at each fire, one watching forward and one watching the other fires to see that no shadows passed between them. As I came closer, I saw that my expectations were correct. There were three guards at each post. All had bows or muskets.

I picked a point halfway between two fires and crawled, expecting an arrow or a musket ball in my back at any moment. When I was close to the guards' line of sight, I took a rock from my pocket and hurled it at a bush far to one side. The technique is a dangerous one; it distracts watchers, but it also makes them alert and suspicious. As soon as I threw, I scuttled forward. Someone shouted "What's that?" Someone else walked forward with a torch and a bow, then said, "Probably a rabbit." I began to breathe again.

I stood when I felt safe enough, which was perhaps fifteen feet farther than I needed to crawl. The next part was easier. The camp was a ring of fires about a ring of tents, and the tents circled a central pavilion that was larger and grander than any of the others. A number of warriors slept in their cloaks near each bonfire. I padded about, careful not to come too close to any light, until I found a thin fellow who had needed to relieve himself in the middle of the night. I relieved him of his cloak, his helmet, and his life.

I sat by the thin man's body for almost half an hour. If I tried to glorify myself in the telling, I would say that I watched to see if he had been missed, to learn the pattern of the sentries' tours, to discover whether Komaki was truly in that central tent. Perhaps I did these things, but mostly I hugged myself and wished I did not stink so badly of fear and self-disgust. Who would mourn the thin man's death?

My left leg began to go to sleep. I waited until no guards were walking near me, then strolled in the stolen helmet and cloak to the back of the largest pavilion. I heard no sound from inside it and saw no light. I glanced around. Almost all of the soldiers by the campfires were asleep. No one watched me. There were no guards at any particular tent, but this one's size and location suggested it was the one I sought. I stayed in the tent's shadow for another moment, letting my eyes adjust as best they could. Then I bent down, lifted the side wall, and rolled under.

My first thought was that I had guessed right. I lay on a thick carpet, such as would be found in a duke's quarters and never in a storage tent. Then light from a suddenly opened lantern almost blinded me. By the tent's entrance, a tall dark man dressed in black held the lantern high in one hand and laughed. A shorter, blond-bearded man sat on a cot close to him.

I brought my left hand up to shield my eyes from the glare while my right flicked a throwing dart from my belt. The laughing man stepped aside, still laughing, and I saw him then. Though he was as tall as any Kond, his skin and his eyes were as dark as mine. His hair was tied back, and I saw that it receded slightly from his temples. There were age lines on his brow and about his eyes, and his strong jaw seemed to carry a hint of extra flesh, though maybe that was only my imagination. He said, "Hello, Izla. Fancy meeting you here."

I nodded and answered as calmly as I could, "A surprise for us both, Rifkin."

༈ 19 ༈

GROMANDIEL
VALLEY

THE BLOND MAN appeared to have been awakened by the lantern. He wore an expensive mail vest over an equally expensive purple shirt. His nose was a cruel beak, and though I tried, I saw no resemblance to Kivakali. "That's Komaki?"

"Yes."

"Don't let him give the alarm."

Komaki glared. "I'll do as I—"

"Patience," I said. "This is more complicated than you imagine." I knew that was true, for it was more complicated than I understood.

Komaki said, "Rifkin, I'm paying you—"

I laughed.

As Komaki looked at me, my other self said, "For my services. I agreed to protect you, and to help you against the witches. That's what I'm doing. Now, be quiet."

Komaki nodded, and without warning, came up from the bed with a dagger in his fist. I watched from my place on the floor as a hand I knew very well slapped the Duke's dagger

171

aside. The other hand closed around Komaki's throat. "My masters would be amused to hear that I had to destroy you in order to save you, Komaki. Be quiet, and be still. If you speak without my permission, I will tear out your tongue. If any of your limbs moves more than an inch, I will crush every bone in it. If you stand, I will snap your spine. If you think of anything to do that I have not mentioned, I will simply kill you if I have no time to be creative. I will kill you very painfully if I do have time. You may nod once, slowly, if you understand me."

Komaki's lips began to curl in rage.

"If I think you're being stupid, I will kill you now. The Lords of Moon Isle do not ally themselves with fools."

Komaki nodded once, slowly.

I said, "A stay in my body has not made you kinder, Izla." He glanced at me. "I'm used to being Rifkin now."

"I'm still used to it. The transfer of minds was more permanent than you thought."

He shrugged. "I should never have rushed the ritual, I suppose, but the rebels hardly left us time. You don't sound like old, stupid Rifkin, though. You sound like me."

I squinted and stood up cautiously. He let me. I said, "Southerners. You can't tell them apart."

He laughed. "You see? Old Rifkin was a loyal fellow, but he had no wit."

Our memories did not match. I stood there, trying to sort the possibilities of what had happened that last day in Istviar when Izla Seaprince, Lord of the Ladizhar Sea, asked his most trusted guard as a final act of duty to exchange bodies for the few days it would take to flee to the country's border.

"You haven't understood yet, have you?" my other self said. "I knew the truth when you saw me and immediately called me by name. Old Rifkin would have stared for half an hour while he puzzled that out."

"I'm Rifkin," I said.

"Names," said my other, tossing one hand in the air to dismiss the matter. "They mean nothing. What basis do you have for identity?"

"My memories are Rifkin's."

"So are mine, old friend. And Izla's, as well. Aren't yours?"

They were not, but I tried to keep my face impassive.

"You don't trust me." He smiled, as if speaking to a child, then laughed. "Of course not. I wouldn't trust me. So I don't."

"I'm Rifkin," I repeated.

"You're neither," he said. "Not Rifkin. Not Izla. In a sense, there are four people taking part in our conversation. There's you, who think yourself Rifkin. There's me, Izla. But there still lurks in this—" he tapped his chest—"Rifkin's body, the mind of the true Rifkin, and I imagine Izla lies in that body, eh?" He smiled when I shook my head. "But that's a simplification. You're the synthesis of both Rifkin and Izla, as am I."

I watched him smile, and it was like watching myself in a distorted mirror, though I hadn't seen that face in a mirror for several years. "I've had to be, to survive since I . . . since we were dethroned. Old Rifkin was always a simple fellow. It was easy to get him to give in to my will, so often that he hardly exists in this body. But in surrendering, he became part of me. His memories are mine, just as his body is mine. His reflexes are mine. Sometimes when I wake in the middle of the night, his fears are mine. I'm not Izla anymore, not the Izla you knew. And I'm certainly not Rifkin, though I keep his name."

I wanted to kill him for saying these things, perhaps because I suspected, no, knew they were true. The original Rifkin was a memory in Rifkin Spirit's mind. How much longer would I survive in Izla's body, if the first Rifkin could not survive in his own?

I tensed like a novice. Rifkin saw it and smiled. "This body has been a killing implement for thirty-five years, Rifkin-myself. You may have trained my body every day you've worn it, but it still will not equal this one."

"I'm younger than you are now," I said.

"And I envy you that," he said. "Almost as much as I envy your witch blood."

"Why did you become a Spirit?"

"I had to sell my skills somewhere. Why do you serve the witches?"

"One saved my life."

"So?"

"It means something to me."

He grinned. "And to me, as well. It means, my more than brother, that we will rule this world soon."

"Oh?"

"I rise quickly through the Spirits' ranks. Rifkin's skill and Izla's wits are an almost unbeatable combination. Now, with you adding Izla's power and doubling his wit—"

"No," I said.

"You need more time to think about this. I understand. Perhaps there's still a bit of Rifkin in you." He studied me. "These names are too confusing. Shall I be Izlarifkin and you, Rifkinizla?"

I wanted to cry "Never!" and throw something in his face. I had listened to too many tales of heroes when I was young. I nodded at him. "Sounds better than Big Rif and Little Rif. You proably wouldn't want to be Little Rif, anyway."

He glanced at me, then grinned. "No, Rifkinizla. I wouldn't."

"You speak freely in front of Komaki."

"He doesn't understand Ladizhan."

"I see," I said. "And what of the witches in the castle?"

"What about them?"

"Would you save them?"

"You're the only witch I want, Rifkinizla."

"They could be useful."

"Or a hindrance. It would attract too much attention to us, if we tried to turn Komaki from his purpose."

"But—"

"Forget your pets. The Spirits are more powerful than any band of witches. I'll serve Moon Isle until I rule it." He smiled fondly at me. "But I'll protect you."

"You're too kind."

"It's interesting, watching you. It's almost like seeing a favorite suit of clothing altered to fit another. I'm almost jealous."

"Izlarifkin," I said, nearly choking on my part of the name, "I intend to protect the people in Castle Gromandiel."

"You needn't, now."

"I especially need to, now."

"Why?"

"A vow."

"Odd." He stroked his chin. I tried to decide if that reminded me of Izla or myself, then realized it was characteristic of Talivane.

"What?" I asked.

"Old Rifkin was a loyal sort, and very stupid, but he wasn't a fool."

"Rifkin always understood duty," I said. "Why else did he serve Izla so well?"

"Because it was easier than doing anything else, my brother. Rifkin always suspected that I, the Izla I, had dear Mother killed. He never acted. Why?"

I stared, but he did not choose to acknowledge my anger.

"Let us stroll through our memories together, my self. Rifkin feared Izla, for Rifkin feared witches."

"I didn't," I whispered. Perhaps I only thought it.

"He told himself that it was important to spare our city from further dissent during a time of civil crisis, so he never spoke his suspicions."

"That was valid, at the time. There were no better—"

"Perhaps," Rifkin Spirit said. "But Rifkin's greatest fear was that Izla's existence was his fault, a result of a dalliance with the Sea Queen before he met his wife. And we both know that's true, don't we, my father, my brother, my self?"

I nodded dumbly. I had told Naiji that my son was dead, and I had not elaborated, thinking all my sons were dead. I did not tell her that I thought I had killed the last one when I took over his body.

"Let the Rifkin in your mind sleep, my brother. You do not need him anymore. You are not him. You're Rifkinizla, now. You've always known that. Acknowledge it."

I looked into his eyes, my eyes. I had not known that dark eyes could be flecked with black. He smiled at me, and something in me said that I had borne Rifkin's sense of honor for too long, carried his sense of guilt for too many deaths.

And perhaps, I realized then, old Rifkin was a simpler man than I remembered. I should have understood everything much sooner than this. He played with me. One fact told him as soon as he saw me that I was only Rifkin, and never Izla, and that was that I carried steel weapons rather than bronze.

I let my shoulders slump as if surrendering to him. I said, "You ... You're right." I shook my head slowly as I studied the ground. "Whatever I am now, I'm partially Izla. Or his child." I reached up to the back of my neck to rub it, as though it ached from many burdens. "How else," I asked, finding the iron pin in my hair and whipping it at the Spirit's chest, "could I trick you so easily?"

He twisted, but the pin still took him high in his right shoulder, almost under the clavicle. His right hand had gone to his belt for a dart as soon as I had acted. My pin slowed him.

I leaped aside, shaking the borrowed cloak from my shoulders, for it would only encumber me. As I moved, I threw a handful of dirt from my pocket at the Spirit's eyes.

Komaki watched desperately, trying to decide what the Spirit would do if he intervened too soon. I had seen the Duke's responses to Rifkin Spirit's threat, so I doubted he would stay quiet for long. During that moment when I might have attacked my other self, I kicked Komaki's left temple to win a few more minutes of privacy.

Rifkin had cleared the dirt from his eyes. He said, "You might have fled."

"I didn't come here to flee."

"You still hope to save those witches?"

I nodded.

He laughed. "Yes, you're definitely Rifkin, for all that you wear my body."

"Thank you," I said. I wondered if he could use his right arm. When he snapped a throwing dart at me, I learned he could. It snagged my jacket as I spun. I continued the spin, flipping my last three darts at him and then finishing with a side kick at his injured arm. He parried with a forearm blow, which left his waist open. I snatched his weapons belt and pulled. We both tumbled to the ground.

I had hoped to counter his skill by getting in close, where we would fight like animals rather than Artists. The result was that his strength gave him the advantage. He shoved back at me, throwing me several feet away. His belt, which I still held in my left hand, came with me. He was not weaponless now, but I had his sword, his knife, and his darts. I doubted he had much else hidden on him.

He kicked at me from his crouch. I whipped the belt at his leg, snagging it. He slashed downward with a dagger that he had worn somewhere. Treacherous fellow. I released the belt, and he tried to stand. The belt served as a snare about his ankles, and he fell again. I kicked him in the head, hard. He fell against a camp table, knocking it down, and lay sprawled as if unconscious.

My edge in battling every Spirit I had encountered had been that they did not expect Izla to fight well. I never thought Izla himself would fall for the same reason.

I should have killed him. I wanted to kill him, but I had killed too many people in the last few days, and this one was myself. If there was still an Izla in my skull who might someday win, perhaps the Rifkin in his would wake again.

I turned to Komaki, and Rifkin's foot caught mine, pitching me. His knife opened my jacket and the bandages beneath it. He snarled, "Surrender, brother."

I tugged my axe from my belt. He tried to take me during that moment, but I had already drawn my own knife. When he lunged, I slashed his forearm.

His face bled from one of my last throwing darts. Its trail told that it had skipped across his cheek, sliced his ear, and gone. A second one was caught in his coat. It did not appear to have touched him. The third must have missed him entirely.

"They're doomed," he said, referring to the folk in the castle. "So are you, if you persevere."

"Never." I thought of the bear, and brought my axe up toward his groin. He caught it with his dagger to deflect it. I stabbed for his torso, but then his foot drove into my testicles.

Free me, Izla whispered. *I will save you.*

"No!" I threw the axe at Rifkin's head. He raised his arm to intercept it, which only resulted in the ruin of the arm. I buried my knife in his side.

Kill him, Izla said. *Kill him now.*

"I can't even kill you, you damned thing. Why should I kill myself?" It seemed to make sense at the time.

I limped to Komaki and slapped him until he woke. Perhaps I should have tried to be quieter, but no guards had investigated yet. I suspected that Rifkin Spirit's orders were not to intervene unless he demanded it, no matter what anyone heard. And perhaps no one had heard anything, for we had fought with little noise, as we had been trained when we were a fishing village boy on White Mountain.

When Komaki's eyes fluttered open, I said, *"I'm* Rifkin." I shook him again. "Rifkin. Say it."

"Rifkin?"

"Right. Not him." I pointed at Rifkin Spirit. "Me. Not him. Rifkin."

"Rifkin. I . . . I understand."

"Good. Understand this. I saw your fear of that thing that wears my name, my . . ." I shook my head to clear it. "My name. You see what I've done to it, here in the heart of your camp."

He nodded.

"I could kill you now, Komaki, but I need you alive. I need you alive to . . ." I shook my head again, trying to remember. ". . . to order your soldiers away from here. Understand that? That's the only thing I need you for. Will you do that?"

He nodded too quickly.

"Good," I said. "Because if you do not, I will come back for you, Komaki, and I will kill you. Then I'll find whoever rules this army after you, and I'll tell that person to take your people home. I would rather not come back again. The person with my name will seem your best friend in the world, if you make me come back for you. Do you understand me, Komaki?"

This time his nod was convincing.

"Good." I put him to sleep with a nerve pinch and turned to go.

Rifkin watched me.

"You're hard to knock out," I said.

He smiled slowly, hiding pain. "You're not an easy opponent, yourself. I thought I kicked your balls."

"You did."

He nodded, seeing that I also hid pain. "Yes. You're old Rifkin."

"You could've killed me while I spoke with Komaki."

He smiled again.

"Why didn't you?"

He shrugged and winced. "You didn't kill me while I lay here."

"So?"

"Maybe a bit more of old Rifkin lives in me than I thought."

"Oh."

"Enough to tell you this: You spared me, I spared you. Go, now. If I recover, we're even."

I nodded. "Even. What about the Duke?"

"I'll tell him that I can protect him, but he won't believe me, not now. Did you kill all the Spirits I sent?"

I turned over a hand, palm up, and let him read whatever he wished in the gesture. "They're dead."

"All?"

"Probably. We even caught Chifeo."

"Who?"

I smiled. "Your masters don't tell you everything, Rifkin Spirit."

I slipped under the tent wall and into the night.

✺ 20 ✺

CASTLE
GROMANDIEL

WHEN I SAY that I slipped into the night, I mean that I slipped into darkness, and when I say that, I mean that my mind became a place as quiet and as dark as the cloudy night. If my body managed to match my mind, that may explain my escape from Komaki's camp. As I left our besiegers behind me, several tents exploded into flame, telling me that someone had decided to try the trick with owls and clay firepots. The ensuing confusion certainly helped me. Besides, no one was watching for anyone sneaking out of the camp and toward the castle. Deserters would go anywhere but Castle Gromandiel.

This doesn't explain how I passed the ring of bonfires, where the guards, in their confusion, probably shot at every hint of shadow. But then, I also can't account for the wound across my buttocks that, Naiji told me later, had to have been caused by a musket ball. I have dazed memories of walking and falling often and in agony. I had functioned after Rifkin Spirit's kick because I had to. That might also be why I ignored the fact that one of my eyes was almost swollen shut, that my nose dripped blood onto my split lower lip, that my ribs only hurt me when I breathed.

My next coherent memory is of standing in front of Gromandiel's gate shouting, "It's Rifkin, damn you! I've saved your stupid asses, now get this goat-buggering door open before I get mad!"

Feschian probably thought this was an unlikely ruse for Komaki to try in hopes of gaining admittance. Someone brought me in, I know, because my next recollection is of lying on a rough bed in the dining room infirmary and Naiji saying "Yes, everyone likes Rifkin's toy boat, now be a good boy and drink your broth."

"Toy boat?" I said.

"I don't know where it is, Rifkin. Sorry. Drink for Naiji-waiji, okay?"

"Are you crazy?"

"Rifkin!" She dropped her wooden bowl on the floor and threw her arms around me. "You're all right!" She was crying and laughing at the same time.

"I don't know," I said. "Toy boat?"

"You kept babbling about—"

I shook my head, which didn't hurt too much. "Please. I think I don't want to know."

"You were very cute."

"Rifkin Cutie. Lucky me."

She nodded. "You're very lucky. Now sit back and drink your broth."

"You spilled it."

"I wouldn't do that," she said, then glanced down and saw the bowl. "Oops. I'll fetch more. You rest." She nodded to herself, then threw herself on me again for another hug and a kiss. "Oh, my," she said a few minutes later. "I think you are much recovered."

"If this was a more private place, I'd show you how much." I watched her walk away, and noted that it was a very good thing to be able to watch her walk away, especially knowing that she would walk back. Then I fell asleep.

I knew it was night when I woke because the room was lit with candles. Sivifal sat near me. "Was I babbling?" I asked.

She shook her head.

"Good. How's your sister?"

"Better."

"She'll recover?"

"Maybe."

"I hope she does."

After a moment the red-headed woman said "Thank you."

"For what?"

"I don't know. But you came saying you'd saved us, and then Komaki left."

"When?"

"This morning."

"Excellent." I reached out for a mug of water. Sivifal came near to help me, but I shook my head. "I'm fairly strong."

Sivifal nodded. "Naiji said you were tougher than you look. She said that now she's rested, she'll try to speed your healing when you wake."

"Zowie."

Sivifal glanced at me. "Zowie?"

"Well, it's a better thing to say than 'toy boat,' wouldn't you think?"

Sivifal nodded. "To be sure. How did you convince Komaki to leave?"

"I appealed to his nobler instincts."

"I didn't know he had any nobler instincts."

"Neither did he."

She smiled a little, then said, "I'll fetch Naiji."

"For the healing?"

She smiled a little more. "Yes."

"Zowie." As she stood, I said, "Wait. Help me up."

She got me to my feet, and I shuffled to my old room. I was wearing a robe that depicted purple, gold, scarlet, and indigo songbirds. Its quality of understated elegance suggested that it was another of Talivane's hand-me-downs. I carried my weapons belt in barely responsive hands.

I was about to pass Naiji's door on my way to my own when I heard her voice behind me. "You can step right in there, stranger."

I turned around slowly because that was easier than looking over my shoulder. "Naiji. You were following me."

She nodded.

"I suppose I dazzle you with my powers of deduction."

"Actually, stranger, it's hardly your powers of deduction that I'm interested in, just now."

"Oh," I said, and reached a hand for her door. When she nodded again, I opened it.

I noted that it was a sumptuous bedroom of the sort I expected Naiji to have, and that the bed, which was large and covered with quilts, looked very soft. I shuffled toward it, set my weapons belt on one corner, shucked the robe and let it drop, then fell forward.

"What grace," Naiji said. "What style."

"Heal me, sweet vision," I said. "Heal me all night long." Then I fell asleep again.

Something was doing very nice things to my thigh as I woke. I thought I should look to see what it was, but that might scare it away. I lay still while it moved higher up my leg. I looked down, and Naiji grinned wickedly at me.

"I don't exactly feel healed," I said, "but I'm not complaining."

"You also aren't concentrating," Naiji said.

"I am."

"On healing."

"On what? Oh. That."

"You've got to help me, Rifkin. Think of something warm inside you."

"I'd rather think of something warm inside you."

"Rifkin!"

"Yes, Lady."

She began to peel bandages away. I saw how many I wore and said, "I don't see why Sivifal bothered to put me in the robe."

"Because she thought that if anyone else saw your cute little buttocks, you wouldn't have reached my room."

"That's understandable."

"Rifkin!"

"Yes, Lady."

I tried to focus on my wounds as things independent of my body. The warmth began to grow again. I wondered if Talivane's lightning was anything like whatever it was that Naiji and I shared. Fire seemed to race through us both, and when I finally entered her, the world faded in a flare of light.

It continued as a simple game of pleasure. I don't know how or when it became something more, but at one point I said, "I love you, Naiji," and she said, "Yes. Thank you." And later, when we both lay in sheets damp with shared sweat, she said, "I love you, Rifkin Freeman," and she hugged me tighter.

After a while, I said, "How did it go?"

"Wonderfully."

"Not that. The day."

"Oh. What do you remember?"

"Almost nothing since leaving Komaki. Tents burning, which I first thought I'd imagined."

Naiji touched my nose, perhaps for the pleasure of doing so, smiled, and said, "You made a horrible ruckus at the gates."

"I remember a little of that. Nothing after."

"Feschian brought you in. She was upset. I think she likes you." Naiji kissed my cheek. "Sivifal and I took turns caring for you. There really isn't much to say. Komaki left soon after sunrise."

"Who sent the owls with the firepots?"

"Feschian."

"I should've guessed. How's Talivane?"

"Better."

"I have to talk to him."

Naiji snuggled closer. "In the morning."

"No." I sat up. "Now."

"No," she said again, suddenly urgent. "Please."

"It's important."

"I'm sure. But not now, Rifkin. I beg you."

"Why?"

"I can't tell you." She began to cry into her hands.

I stroked her hair. "Why?"

"I can't tell you! Please, Rifkin. Just wait. Please."

I shook my head and tried to explain. "It's about Komaki. He left because I threatened him, told him what I would do if he stayed. So he went. But he won't forget about us. He'll be back, better prepared. All I've won is time, and if we waste that—"

"Talk to Talivane in the morning. Not tonight," Naiji whispered. "Don't make me choose between you, Rifkin. Please?" Her eyes were wide and moist.

"I'm sorry." I stood and found the robe.

"Rifkin?"

"Yes?"

"If I tell you . . . what he does, will you promise to wait?"

"I'll listen. But I won't wait all night."

"Decide that later. Agreed?"

I nodded. "As you wish." Her pale hair had fallen about her face, so I brushed it back behind her ears. She kissed my wrist as my hand passed by her.

"He's in his room with the last Spirit. He practices magic. Magic of . . . of passion. To increase his power. Like when I healed you tonight, but different."

I think I understood then. Still, I said, "How do you mean?"

"It . . ." She bit her lip.

"Yes?" I insisted, beginning to hate her for her part in this, even if I did not know what that part was. "How?"

"His lovers die."

I turned to face the wall and tried futilely to meditate. I remembered the screams that I had heard each night. Perhaps there should not be a hierarchy of the types of death, since all are routes to the Black Shark or the White Lady. So I told myself while I lay there, aware of Naiji and not caring whether she remained in the room or left.

I tried to think calmly and order my priorities. I must save Naiji, yet she would not save herself unless Talivane and her people left the castle. And they would not leave unless Talivane left, for they thought him their salvation. And Talivane brought prisoners to him in the night, couched with them, and slew them in the act of pleasure to increase his power. I wondered if he made them trust him first by promising their freedom. Perhaps he drugged them. Perhaps he knew some way to seize their will and make them think what he pleased. Perhaps—

"Rifkin?" Naiji whispered, lying close behind me, yet not touching me. In spite of our distance, a matter of inches, I could sense the tension in her body.

"Yes?" I said.

"I meant it when I . . ."

"Yes?"

"When I named you Freeman. You may leave me."

"Is that your wish, Lady?"

"No! Oh, Rifkin, no!"

"Oh. You prefer that I stay?"

"Please, Rifkin. Don't do this to me."

"Do what, Lady?"

She clawed at my shoulder to turn me. Her hair was wild about her face, and her eyes and her nose were swollen and red. "I love you, Rifkin."

"And quite competently, Lady."

She began to cry again.

"How many have you two killed to learn your tricks of love and power, Lady?"

"Rifkin, I'm not part—"

"Did I say it matters?" I turned back to the wall.

"I didn't know..."

"Didn't know what? That magicless folk are people too? Or do I make a false assumption there? Perhaps you practiced your arts on witches too."

She said quietly, "I didn't know what happened in Talivane's room, Rifkin."

I shrugged. "As you say, Lady."

"I didn't! I helped Talivane to soothe the others before he took them away, but he always had me wait in his sitting room while he—" She gasped. "While he..."

"You knew what happened in there, Lady. You've said as much."

She was silent for a moment, then spoke. "I knew, Rifkin. Talivane told me. Two evenings ago. He wanted my help, to..." She started to sob again.

I touched my fingers to the tears at the corners of her eyes. "To what?"

"To learn the tricks, Rifkin. He increased his power that way, by exercising his skills while he played at making love. But it wasn't enough. He thought he could learn to draw more from the act if he could find a woman to study the other half of sex and love and..." She met my gaze and finished, "... and death. He wanted us to be students together, to teach each other what we learned from killing our victims."

"He might have studied without killing. As you say you have."

"He did. He didn't learn as much that way, not as quickly. And the study of healing would never have taught him..."

"Yes?"

"To kill with the act, Rifkin. To kill with love, or lust, if you prefer."

"That's insane."

"So's Talivane," she said.

"And you stand by him."

"He's my brother."

I put my palm against her cheek, and she pressed her hand against mine. I said, "Is this true? About the killing?"

"Yes."

I stared at her. "Why? Why would Talivane—"

"He says it's the ultimate source of power, for a witch, anyway."

I thought about what I had learned of sex, emotion, and magic. "How—"

"There are books in the library, Rifkin. Old books about the days when the practice of magic was common. There were witches who used humans as though they were dogs, in those days. When Talivane looked for a way to make use of his knowledge, he hit on this plan. If he could master the skills to win enough power, he could stop Komaki, could marry Janiavy, could—"

"He could do anything," I said.

"Almost," she agreed.

"And what would your people think of this?"

"He would never tell them the source of his power. The practice was always despised, and even at the worst times of the Empire, it was illegal."

"Would you tell your people what he does?"

I thought she might cry again, but she shook her head, saying "No. He's my brother, Rifkin. But I refused to help him after I knew what he was doing."

"I see."

"I knew that his prisoners died. I just didn't know how. Before I knew, I thought the killings would help us all, because I did know the deaths heightened Talivane's skills. But I'm not making excuses. I just didn't know the true reasons."

"I believe you," I said at last.

"And forgive me?"

"What am I, a saint?"

"Please, Rifkin."

I closed my eyes and nodded.

"What'll you do?" Naiji asked.

"The only thing I can." I got out of bed, and thinking of the task ahead of me, looked at my robe in dismay.

"Nothing will deter you?"

"I don't know about that," I said. "Where can I find some pants?"

21

CASTLE GROMANDIEL

I DRESSED IN the blue and burgundy clothes that I had worn before. Naiji put on another hunting outfit, this one all in indigo. "My boots?" I asked.

"In the infirmary, probably. You don't want to talk about this?"

"No."

"I'm coming with you." She pulled on thigh-length black leather boots, then buckled on her saber.

"And here I thought you just liked exotic sleepwear."

"I'm coming with you," she repeated quietly.

I nodded, and we walked side by side through the dark halls to the infirmary. Sivifal, resting in a soft chair, woke when we entered and smiled at us. "A good healing?" she whispered.

I shrugged, a little embarrassed, and Sivifal smiled. Naiji said, "Where're his boots?"

Sivifal pointed. They stood beneath an empty cot, so I went and put them on. As I did, I slipped another pin from the many sheaths sewn into the right boot top. Then I brushed my hand through my hair as if smoothing it, and hid the pin there.

Naiji and I went from the dining room infirmary to the bell tower. I found the rope for the clapper and rang it twice. By the time we descended to the courtyard, most of the castle's inhabitants were waiting for us, excepting the children and the wounded. Avarineo and Fat Cat and two others were naked but for cloaks and boots and weapons. Most people had dressed in bits of hastily chosen clothing and armor. Feschian was one of the few who had managed to dress completely, though I suspected she had fastened her breastplate as she ran there. She called, "What is it, Rifkin?"

"Komaki's returning," I said. "We must leave this place tonight."

"Oh?" said Talivane, resplendent in yellow silk trimmed with sable. "Our birds brought no word of warning."

"It's true just the same. Or will be."

"Ah," said Talivane. "You're a seer, now. How nice of you to tell us your fancies, Rifkin."

"Listen, Talivane—"

"Lord Talivane," he corrected.

"Talivane," I said, "try not to be such a pompous fool, eh?"

"Careful, Rifkin." He gestured with his hand like a school-teacher might. For him, it was a subtle warning. "Only the fact that you're my sister's pet—"

"No more," I said. "She freed me."

He glanced at Naiji, and after a moment, she nodded. "Interesting," said Talivane. "I understand how you would grow weary of Rifkin's simple wit, but—"

"I love him," she said quietly.

"You're tired, my sister. Perhaps you should go to bed. Perhaps everyone should go back to bed."

"No," I said. "Everyone should pack, immediately, to leave this castle as soon as we can."

"Will you never stop proposing that?"

I shook my head.

"Do you know what I think, Rifkin?"

"No," I said. "I don't even know that you do think."

"I think that you're in Komaki's employ. I think he saw that he could never take this castle, so he had you meet with him last night. Then he had you beaten a little, so we would suspect nothing, and he went away, expecting you to convince us to flee from here. To flee into Komaki's trap."

I glanced at the others before I spoke. Avarineo listened with wrinkles of puzzlement on his face. Fat Cat watched me with some suspicion. The remaining people might as well have worn masks.

"No," I said. "I threatened the Duke, and he left. But he's not the sort to be ruled by threats. He'll return soon, with more warriors or more Spirits. Maybe both. We should go while we can."

"You threatened him?" Talivane said skeptically.

I nodded.

"You crept into his camp, asked him to leave, and returned here, almost unscathed."

"Almost unscathed," I said. "I like that. If I ever write about this, I'll tell it that way. Almost unscathed, Rifkin returned—"

"Enough," Talivane said. "Don't wake us again, or you die."

"Talivane," I said slowly. "Don't make me tell your secrets to your people."

"I have no secrets from my people."

"Oh?" I scratched the back of my neck as though I was perfectly comfortable before him. "What of those prisoners who die in your quarters in the middle of the night? Do you think we're all such fools as to think you an inept interrogator?"

"I kill the prisoners when I have finished with them," Talivane said, watching me with increasing suspicion, "because they would be a threat to us all if allowed to live. Everyone knows that Spirits cannot be turned aside from their targets."

I laughed. "Come now, Talivane!" I stepped forward and clapped his cloaked shoulder. "The dungeons here would hold a hundred Spirits for twice as many years."

He glared at my hand as he spun away from me. "You dare—"

"Talivane," I said. "Most of the good people here think as little of magicless folk as the magicless folk think of us. Yet I imagine no one would respect or obey you if they knew how you intend to gain—"

"Stop, Rifkin. I begin to grow very tired of warning you."

I nodded. "And I grow very tired of being warned. But we must abandon this castle while we can. If you disagree, I'll speak the truth about you, so each can decide what he will."

Dovriex said, "It's silly to fight among ourselves."

Naiji said, "Perhaps in the morning—"

"Tonight," I said.

Talivane shook his head to demand silence. "I will not be threatened, Rifkin."

"I don't threaten, Talivane. I advise." More gently, I said, "Accept advice from others too. Feschian, could we survive another attack?"

Talivane glanced at her. Feschian met his gaze and said "No. We could not."

Talivane said, "Komaki doesn't know that."

I said, "He knows we couldn't survive several more attacks. He's not a fool."

"This castle is my home," Talivane said. "It has been the home of my people for fourteen hundred years. I will not leave it."

"Fine," I said. "Stay." I hesitated, then said, "I don't want anyone to ever think I treated you unfairly, Talivane. Permit me two statements before you decide whether to silence me."

Naiji said warningly, "Rifkin . . ."

Talivane laughed. "Speak your two statements."

"This is the first. If I were you, I would not try to silence me."

He laughed louder. "You are an amusing fellow, Rifkin. And your second?"

"Your people believe you to be a harsh but essentially honorable man. If they decide with no more information than they have, they'll choose to stay and die here with you. So, if you won't leave, I must tell things that you would prefer I did not. It's the only way they may truly decide for themselves."

He shook his head. "You're a fool, Rifkin."

I raised my hand. "I wouldn't—"

"You think I'll stand here and let you speak your lies—"

"Truth," I said.

Talivane told Naiji, "He condemns himself."

She whispered, "Don't. Please, Talivane, don't."

He looked at me. "Your decision, Rifkin. Speak your lies and die. Or apologize and let us all sleep."

"No, Talivane," I said wearily. "Your decision." I breathed deeply, for I was very frightened. I turned to the others, to

Dovriex and Feschian and Sivifal and Avarineo and Fat Cat and the rest whose names I still did not know. I said, "Your lord studies—"

"Farewell, fool," Talivane said, smiling his satisfaction. His hands flared with lightning, but it did not dart toward me. It burst around Talivane, enclosing him in a sphere of dancing sparks. Within it, he twitched and danced and burned. When Talivane finally crumpled to the ground, the lightning died with him.

Naiji may have cried too much in the last two days. She only stared and whispered, "Talivane. Talivane." Her fists were tight at her side.

Feschian turned to me with her unsheathed sword and spoke for the others. "What happened?"

I shrugged, though I wanted to puke.

Dovriex said, "What was this truth for which Talivane died?"

I managed to say, "It doesn't matter now." Then I did puke.

Feschian steadied me. I appreciated that, even more than the fact that I had seen her draw her sword the instant before Talivane began his last spell. I suspected that meant Feschian liked me, but since her gesture had come too late, I would never embarrass her by mentioning it.

One of the witches I did not know said to Naiji, "You're Gromandiel now. What should we do?"

Naiji studied me, and I wondered how much she suspected. After a moment she said softly, "We pack and leave."

"To where?" asked Avarineo.

"Away," she whispered.

"Away sounds good, mistress. I will go pack for away." She looked around. "Am I Lady Gromandiel?"

"Yes," said several.

"Then why haven't you begun to pack? We go in twenty minutes."

Fat Cat said, "But the dead—"

"Would all prefer that we continue to live, I suspect."

He nodded. "Yes, Lady." He and most of the others hurried away.

Feschian had rolled Talivane's body onto a cloak. She asked Naiji, "Pardon, Lady, but where should we take him?"

Naiji looked around the overgrown courtyard. "He wanted to stay here. Our home. Take him..." She looked up at the bell tower and said, "Up there, Captain. He would like that."

I started to complain, then told myself that Talivane was Naiji's brother, and she loved him, whatever he had been, and he had loved her, in his way. I could help carry his corpse up too many stairs, if that would help to ease Naiji's pain.

As I bent to take Talivane's shoulders, Naiji touched mine and said hoarsely, almost forcing herself to speak, "You warned him, at least. Thank you." She left before I could find an answer.

Feschian and I carried Talivane to his resting place. The tower's top was roofed, but its sides were open. The floor was dusty and spattered with bird dung. In the daytime the view encompassed almost all of the valley. "He'll like it here," Feschian said. She knelt by Talivane's head for a moment.

"Perhaps." I only wanted to leave him as quickly as we could.

"This is yours, I think," Feschian said. In her hand she held the charred iron pin that I had slipped into Talivane's cloak when I clapped his shoulder.

I took it from her, then threw it into the night. "If he'd only agreed that we should leave, or even to let me explain—"

Feschian shook her head. "You did what you thought best."

"That doesn't make it easier."

"No." She gripped my arm for a moment. "Will you explain it to Naiji?"

I nodded. "That won't be easy either."

Feschian moved her hand from my arm to my face. "She's lucky." Then she let her hand drop and said, "She could use a little luck. Come on. You heard what the lady said. Twenty minutes."

At the bottom of the stairs, I said, "Two things."

"Talivane died when you gave him the same warning."

I managed to smile a little, though Feschian didn't. I said, "This is safer. Where're Kivakali's rooms?"

"Room," Feschian corrected. "Only three doors past Talivane's, though he never entered it."

"And what of Chifeo? Is he still alive?"

Feschian nodded. "In the dungeons. The only occupant now, excepting rats and lice."

"And the keys?"

"On a peg in the guardroom."

I thanked her and left. I sought Kivakali first, for something had bothered me since I spoke with Rifkin Spirit. Kivakali was in her room, stuffing too many clothes into a large canvas pack. If that meant she intended to join us, I suspected she would throw away half its contents before we had walked for a day. I only said, "Lady Kivakali?"

She glanced up in surprise. "Yes?"

"When you told the Spirits how to enter this castle, did you know they would try to kill Naiji as well as Talivane?"

Her fear of me choked her voice. "I . . ."

"If you lie well enough, I won't say anything of this to anyone."

"N-no. I didn't think . . . that."

"Could've been better," I said. "But that'll do. You're free of him now."

"Yes," she whispered, still not trusting me.

I indicated the heap of clothing. "You needn't pack all that if you plan to return to your father. You could wait for him here."

She shook her head. "My father never treated me well."

"Have the witches?"

"Not Talivane. Not most of them. But—" She glanced at me.

"Dovriex is a good fellow," I said.

She smiled shyly. "Yes."

"You'll come with us, then?"

"No. I'll find a place of my own, I think."

I nodded. "I can understand that." I tried to think of something more to say. I pointed at a stack of dresses. "Take the red. It'll go better with your hair than the pink."

"Do you think so?"

"I don't know. I'm the fellow who's been wearing a brown belt with blue and burgundy."

She took the red, which confirmed my decision to keep the matter of the Spirits a secret.

Chifeo was sleeping when I opened his cell. I spoke his name.

He turned and glanced at me. "Kill me, Seaprince. I will not beg."

I scratched my head. "You amaze me, Chifeo. Two sentences and three stupid ideas. Who were you taking lessons from, Talivane or Avarineo?"

"Huh!" He turned and looked away.

"One," I said, because I had been counting things that night. "I'm not here to kill you. Two. I'm not Izla. Three. If it'll help you stay alive, beg desperately. If you die anyway, you haven't lost anything. And if you live—"

"What do you know of honor?"

"That it can't be summed up in a sentence or two, Chifeo."

He squinted. "Why're you here?"

"To free you."

"Why?"

"The witches are leaving."

He looked around. "You try to trick me."

"No." I watched him stand and walk to the open door.

He stopped. "I can go?"

"Sure."

"Where?"

"Home to the Spirits, if you wish. They'll treat you badly, of course. They aren't fond of failures, or witches."

He thought, then said, "No."

"Or you could come with us."

He stared. "You trust me?"

"No."

"But I can still come with you?"

"Yes."

"Why?"

"Because I am very tired of killing, Chifeo."

"It's easy."

"I know. That's part of the reason I'm tired of it."

"Where are you going?"

"Witchhold," I said.

"It doesn't exist."

I shrugged.

"Who else is going?"

"Whoever wants to."

He nodded. "I'll come too."

In the courtyard the witches waited in traveling clothes. Eight adults on foot, bearing packs. Two adults in stretchers that we would carry. Five sleepy children and two babies in the arms of the oldest children. The kitchen hound. The hearth cat.

Kivakali stood away from the others, waiting while Feschian and Livifal opened the gate. Dovriex saw Kivakali's pack and said, "Will you come with us?"

Kivakali shook her head.

Dovriex took a step forward and said, looking down, "With me, then? For a ways, perhaps?"

She smiled slightly. "For a ways, perhaps."

The front gates opened. Naiji glanced from Chifeo to me and back again. "I'll vouch for him," I said. Naiji nodded. I took her hand, and we set out in search of a myth.

We found it, of course. But that's another story.